UNLOCKING HOPE (SPECIAL FORCES: OPERATION ALPHA)

A FLIPPING LOVE STORY, BOOK 2

LINZI BAXTER

Dear Readers,

Welcome to the Special Forces: Operation Alpha Fan-Fiction world!

If you are new to this amazing world, in a nutshell the author wrote a story using one or more of my characters in it. Sometimes that character has a major role in the story, and other times they are only mentioned briefly. This is perfectly legal and allowable because they are going through Aces Press to publish the story.

This book is entirely the work of the author who wrote it. While I might have assisted with brainstorming and other ideas about which of my characters to use, I didn't have any part in the process or writing or editing the story.

I'm proud and excited that so many authors loved my characters enough that they wanted to write them into their own story. Thank you for supporting them, and me!

READ ON!

Xoxo

Susan Stoker

ZOEY

Zoey wished for running water, but when she twisted the handles to the faucet, only a couple of drops trickled out. Like the last three months, she was out of luck. Instead of leaving and trying to find another foreclosed house, she sat with her back against the wall in the master bedroom.

She checked herself in the broken mirror propped up in the room's corner. She couldn't even run her fingers through her tangled brown hair. Zoey wished she had some makeup to cover the bags under her eyes.

When she'd first ended up on the streets a few months ago, she still did her makeup every morning. Carrying makeup around took up room in her pack, though, and when she had to decide between a few granola bars or foundation, she'd decided on the granola bars. At the thought of food, her stomach growled.

"You're not hungry," she murmured to herself. Zoey reached into her pocket and broke off a small piece of the granola bar. It was stale. She'd stopped looking at expiration dates her second week on the street. At first, she wouldn't have choked down an outdated bar. Now, when it was her only option, it didn't bother her.

The foreclosed house would be her safe haven for a few days. Zoey curled up against the wall and hoped for a few hours of sleep. Paul had told her to use this house for the week. He had a contact at the Bexar County Courthouse. Every so often, he would find out about a home that was empty. She trusted Paul as much as a person could trust anyone living on the streets. However, something about the old man made her take him up on the offer. Maybe it was for the hope of a shower, but that dream had gone out the door when she tried to turn on the water.

Zoey wasn't the first one to stay in the house. The previous squatters had left their trash and crap on the wall. She never understood who would touch their own poop and smear it on a wall. She shook her head and looked around the room. It was bare, the only room with no trash. In addition, it was in the far back of the house. Wires hung out of the outlets, and a single light bulb hung from the ceiling. Like the water, the electrical was off.

The Texas sun beat down on the house. She reached up and wiped the sweat dripping down her face. She smelled. The first few days of being on the street, she worried about her smell, but she no longer even cared what anyone thought. Zoey's only goal was to stay alive until she figured out what to do with the thumb drive in her pocket. Zoey reached in her pocket to make sure it was still there. When they found her, they would torture her until she gave them the information they wanted.

Zoey glanced out the window. The sun was going down. She still wished the window had blinds so she could block out the early-day heat.

The smell in the house had been awful at first, and she'd almost gone back to the homeless shelter in downtown San Antonio. Zoey reached into her bag and pulled out her last bite of granola bar. Today, she would need to leave and find food.

The front door squeaked. Time had run out. She only hoped it wasn't one of Nixson Walker's men. If it was, she didn't plan to go down easy. Living on the streets had taught her a few things, like to shoot first and ask questions second. She knew she should jump out the back window. Nevertheless, if she could take the person down, she could take his cash and have a meal. She reached into her backpack and grabbed her gun. It still felt strange under her fingers. Until a month ago, she'd never imagined owning one or having to use it. She hadn't pulled the trigger yet, but it had helped her out when someone tried to steal her bag three nights ago.

Nixson, her ex-boss, was a ruthless businessman, and he wanted her dead. His men almost succeeded at killing her the night she went on the run. For three months, she had outrun Nixson's men, until now.

Zoey stood on her wobbly legs. Not eating much for the past month had left her body weak. She couldn't remember the last time she'd eaten a real meal. When she'd gone to the homeless shelter, Nixson's men were outside. Paul had given her a box of bars, and she had paced herself, eating one a day for the last week.

With a gun pointed at the door, she waited for the men who planned to kill her. A man opened the door, dressed in a polo and jeans. He was well over six feet tall and muscular, with sandy-blond hair. His eyes were a piercing blue. She noticed them because when they landed on the gun, they widened in surprise.

"Ma'am, please lower the gun, and we can talk."

"You won't take me back."

When he took a step forward, Zoey closed her eyes and pulled the trigger. The force of the gun firing knocked Zoey on her butt. Her head banged against the wall. She hoped she'd hit him, because that was her only bullet.

"What the fuck? You shot at me." His gruff voice sounded angry.

"You won't take me back." Zoey opened her eyes and peeked at the handsome man sent to bring her back to the boss.

He ran his hand through his hair. "Darling, you're mistaken. I don't plan to take you anywhere. You're squatting in my house."

"Oh." That wasn't good. She'd wasted her only bullet.

He cocked his head to the side. "'Oh' is all you have to say when you shot at me?"

If he called the cops, they would take her to Nixson. He had them all paid off. Zoey reached for her bag and purse. Time to run. "I'm sorry I'm in your house. If you will excuse me, I will be on my way."

The sexy man crossed his arms over his chest. "You shot at me, and you think I'm just going to let you walk out the front door."

Zoey's hands started to shake. She could feel the tears forming in her eyes. She couldn't escape the room unless she walked by him. "Please let me go. You can't call the cops."

"Why can't I call the cops?"

"Because the man after me has them paid off. His men will take me to my old boss and not the police."

"Let's start over. My name is Cole. What is yours?"

"Kate." It was the first name to pop into her head.

His lips twitched as if he knew she'd lied about her name. "Okay, Kate, how about we get some food?" When she started to protest, he held up his hand. "You owe me that after shooting at me."

"Why do you want to take me somewhere to eat?"

He shrugged. "It looks like luck hasn't been on your side lately, and I'm hungry. So let's grab some food, and if you feel you can trust me to help you, we'll go from there."

This all sounded too good to be true. Who would help someone after being shot at? It could be a trap.

Zoey gripped the gun in her hand. He didn't know she was out of bullets. Zoey pointed her weapon in his direction and grabbed her bags from the ground. "Move."

The sexy man listened to her and moved away from the door. She slogged across the room and slipped past him. His cologne was the only nice thing she'd smelled in days. It looked like her time in his house was up anyway. Maybe Paul would know another place she could hide.

Once she cleared the door, she ran down the hall toward the front door. She didn't hear the man's footsteps behind her. The front door was still open, and she continued out the door. She stopped when she saw the Range Rover parked in the driveway. Nixson's men all drove Mercedes-Benz G-Classes. Maybe the man wasn't lying. She didn't trust anyone, though. Everyone lied.

Zoey ran down the sidewalk as fast as her weak legs would take her. She was only a few blocks from the alleyway where Paul slept. The sun was setting, so Zoey hoped he was already there. The neighborhood she walked though was beautiful, and a woman watering her front yard gave Zoey a disgusted look. Zoey didn't blame her.

Why did she have to take a job as a CFO for a

corrupt man? She'd realized too late that the consulting firm was a front. If she'd done some checking instead of just looking at the dollar signs they offered after the first interview, she never would've moved from Dallas to San Antonio. Zoey had left her job working as a financial advisor at Nova Satellite Security, and she'd loved working for the Black brothers. The money at Walker Consulting was all too good, though. Her close friend had told her about the job. Well, Linda used to be her friend. She had no problem working for someone running drugs and extortion. Zoey thought that type of people only existed in the movies; she'd never expected to run into them in real life.

She let out a sigh and looked back to make sure the sexy man wasn't following her. Zoey reached into her pocket and patted the USB drive. It was her only copy of the information, she had made another, but they'd stolen it when she lost half her things at the homeless shelter.

Over the years, she had gone to the gym off and on, but not enough to keep her in shape for this run. Her stomach growled, reminding her she needed food. Her vision was blurry from the exercise and lack of carbs. She looked up at the street signs. *8th Street. One more to go.*

When she turned down the side street to where Paul normally slept, Zoey let out a breath, seeing him crouched near his corner. Paul had been on the streets long enough that most people respected him. Nobody took his corner. Newcomers sometimes tried but would end up beaten by the younger homeless guys. Paul was like everyone's grandfather. If he liked someone, he helped.

As she got closer, she noticed something wasn't right. "Paul?"

He didn't move from his position. She rushed to his side. He was hunched over leaning against the wall. His face was pale, and his eyes were closed. *No. No. No.* When she gently shook him, he groaned and opened his eyes.

"You need to run." His voice was hoarse.

"What happened?"

"They are watching—you need to run."

Zoey knew that coming back to downtown San Antonio had been dangerous, but she couldn't leave Paul. She could only imagine his current condition was because of her. Zoey tried hard to keep the tears at bay. She had cried more in the past few months than she had her entire life.

When she reached forward to grip Paul under his arm, her hand hit something wet. Her eyes burned with tears as she pulled her hand back. *Blood.* "Come on, Paul, we need to get you to the hospital."

"You need to go." His words came out so weak, she almost hadn't heard what he said.

Zoey wouldn't be able to get Paul to a hospital alone. After her first week on the streets, she'd realized Nixson could track her with her phone, so she'd ditched it.

Movement caught her eye to the side. She raced over to a box near the dumpster, where Paul's friend Al usually stayed. Al had a prepaid phone, and Zoey hoped he was under the box. She screamed when a raccoon ran out. She took a couple deep breaths before she glanced inside. She found Al, with a knife sticking out of his chest. His eyes were still open, but the color was gone from his face. This was bad—really bad. There was nothing she could do to help Al. With one last glance, she left his side.

Zoey ran back to Paul. "Hold on, Paul. I'm going to get help."

He started to shake his head. Without waiting for his answer, Zoey raced down the alley. When she was almost to the front, three thugs turned the corner. Zoey inwardly cussed at herself for leaving her gun next to Paul. It wouldn't do much, anyway, since she didn't have any bullets left.

"Zoey, the boss isn't happy with you." Eric, Nixson's second in command, stepped forward. Tweedledee and Tweedledum, his two henchmen, followed close behind.

"I swear I have nothing."

"Boss doesn't care."

Zoey took another step back. She was getting close to where Paul lay on the dirty ground. Glancing from side to side, she looked for something she could use to protect herself. Al had a bat near his makeshift cardboard home.

Eric caught where her eyes landed. "You should have heard the old man squeal as I plunged the knife into his chest. He will not help you. That one"—he pointed toward Paul—"will not last much longer, either. Time's up."

This is bad. But a quick death would be better than letting them take her back to Nixson. Shivers ran down her arms as she thought about the last person she'd seen him torture for talking out of turn. She needed to figure out something quick. If she didn't, Paul might not make it. Zoey wouldn't let the thugs take her without a fight. She dove for the bat. The dirty pavement scraped her arms as she slid toward the only thing that might help her.

She gripped the wooden bat and rolled to the

side as she heard the gun go off. She sprang to her feet, and a loud siren echoed down the street. Eric and his thugs turned to see if they'd been spotted. She used the opportunity to swing the bat at him. With a good hit, Zoey took out his leg. She felt it crack as she made contact. His thugs reached to help him. Zoey ran. She pumped her arms, trying to get away. With a few feet to go before she exited, Zoey felt the grip on her hair.

The people on the sidewalk watched as the men threw her back and her head hit the ground. One of the hired thugs kicked her in the side. She felt her rib crack. She had to blink a few times to get the edge of darkness to go away. No one stopped.

The pain was all she could feel. Eric hobbled back to where she lay on the ground. He had one arm around one of his henchmen and a gun pointed at her. Her eyes were trained on his finger as he slowly squeezed the trigger.

COLE

She fucking shot at him. Cole watched the wildcat race around him and run for the exit of the house. She was skin and bones, and her clothes hung off her body. It was the worry in her steely-gray eyes that made him want to help, though. She'd said her name was Kate, but he knew it was a lie the second the words left her mouth. Everyone lied. At a young age, Cole had honed his ability to tell when someone was fibbing by watching every move his father made.

Kate needed help. She looked like someone on the run, not someone squatting in a house because she was homeless. If he had to guess, someone was after her, and that didn't sit well with him. Not wanting to make her more skittish, Cole gave her a head start as he slowly worked his way down the hallway, taking in every room of his next flip. The sound of the door slamming brought a smile to Cole's face. She could run, but he would catch her.

When she ran past him, he could've used his experience as a Navy SEAL to remove the gun from her hands. Taking the only item that made her feel safe would push her away, and Cole wanted to know everything about her—not only what she is running from, but also what she liked to eat. The dampness in her eyes made him want to kill the person who made her feel scared. Pure fear was what he saw when she rushed by him.

Cole grasped the front door handle, pulled open the door, and welcomed the hot, humid air. It was refreshing compared to the smell in the house. Not wanting another squatter, Cole closed the door and locked the deadbolt. It would hold until tomorrow. He'd planned to change the house locks and make a list of the projects he needed to start, but his instinct told him Kate needed his help. Many missions as a Navy SEAL had taught him to trust his gut, and he didn't plan to stop today. Cole lowered his sunglasses as he walked toward his SUV.

When he reached for the handle, his phone vibrated in his front pocket. He opened the door to his Range Rover and jumped in before pulling out his phone. The name of his business partner and long-time friend, Ian, flashed across the screen. He couldn't help but roll his eyes. Ian and his fiancée, Bella, were supposed to be on vacation for a few days after battling with people trying to kill Bella. She had bought her first flip, a Victorian home, and from the first day, someone kept trying to scare her away by vandalizing the property. When she didn't stop working on the house or sell the project, he attacked her one night. Once the police arrived and questioned the man, who had also vandalized the fireplace, he admitted to burying his sister in the fireplace, along with a million dollars. Bella and Ian thought she was no longer in danger, but then Bella's ex-boss's two kids kidnapped her and took her across the country. Ian and Cole called on the help of friends to save her. Now they were both supposed to be relaxing, not worrying about the house they'd bought.

Cole kept his eyes on Kate while he swiped his finger across the phone to answer the call. "What happened to you being on vacation and not worrying about work?"

Ian chuckled on the other side. "Bella wanted to know if we got the ho—" Ian grunted. "Don't hit me... Okay, we *both* wanted to know if we got the house. It wasn't only Bella."

Bella spit out her questions before Cole could even answer. "Can we salvage the house, or are we going to have to gut everything? I think this will be a good one."

Cole chuckled as he reversed his Range Rover to follow Kate. "To answer Ian's question—yes, we got the house. The house... had lots of surprises."

"Come on, Cole. I need more than that," Bella whined.

His wildcat turned down Conner Street, heading toward downtown San Antonio. "Well, it had squatters in it for a while—poop covered the walls and trash littered the floors. Don't get me going on the smell of fermented vomit." Talking about the smells made his stomach roll. He would need to buy masks before he reentered the house.

Ian sighed. "The house sat empty for well over a year, so I'm not surprised a few people squatted in the home."

Before deciding to bid on the house, he had pulled the liens to see if any were outstanding. Over the past year, the city had issued a few to this property for not keeping the lawn up and for trash lying in the yard. In the next few days, Cole would petition the city to get the outstanding balance down. Their friend Officer Max Anders had told them a few of their officers had been called to the house over the past year for noise and smell complaints. Cole was happy he'd found only one person in the house. Squatters weren't the easiest to deal with. Over the years, they had purchased a few homes with squatters and had to call the police to get the people out. Kate, on the other hand, had bolted. Cole knew he should turn around and head back to the house, but something about the woman pulled him toward her.

"Yeah, poop on the walls and a mess are what I expected, not a woman shooting at me."

"Are you okay?" Bella asked.

"Did you shoot back?" Ian asked at the same time.

He had left his gun in the glove box, but he wasn't sure he would've pulled his gun on the woman, anyway. He could tell by the way her hands shook as she'd held the gun that she wouldn't be a good shot. With a little luck, she might've hit him.

Cole gripped the steering wheel. "No, I didn't shoot back, and no, she didn't hit me." He let out a long sigh. "I think she needs help."

"Is she still in the house?" Ian asked.

"Nope, she ran out, and now I'm following her

down the street." Cole turned down a side street. He wondered where she was headed, because the homeless shelter was the other way. As she ran down the street, she gripped her dirty, loose jeans with one hand and pumped her other arm.

"Have you called Max yet?"

"No, I haven't had a chance. You called the second I walked out the door." Cole couldn't imagine what it would be like to have to sleep on the floor of someone's house and not know if they would come home. He'd spent a lot of his military career sleeping on the floor or ground, but he knew he had a bed to go back to, unlike the wildcat.

"Call him. Don't go after her alone." Ian's voice held concern.

"Don't worry about me. I got this. Her aim is way off, and when she ran by me, she gave me her back. I don't think she's been homeless for long. I think she's on the run."

"Call us tonight and let us know if you need us to come back early."

"Enjoy your time in the cabin. Don't worry about me. Now I'm going to let you go so I can figure out where she headed."

Ian and Bella said bye before he swiped the end button on his phone and dropped it into the console.

When she ran past an elderly woman watering the lawn, the woman narrowed her eyes and shook her head. Cole wanted to keep his distance, so he slowed to a stop and continued to watch her run down the street. She hadn't turned her head once to see if he was following her. When she rounded another corner down a side street, Cole found a parking spot a few feet away from the alley. He put the Range Rover in park and looked around him. He was in the crime-ridden area in downtown known for drugs and prostitution. A dim-lit alleyway was not the best place for Kate or any woman. Cole leaned over his center console, opened his glove box, and grabbed his Glock.

People walked up and down the sidewalks, not paying attention to anything around them, including the woman who turned down the alleyway. Nobody took the time to stop Kate and ask if she needed help. Instead, they walked by her and continued with their day, not giving her an ounce of their attention.

A man dressed in suit pants and a white button-down shirt turned down the side street, flanked by two taller men with short dark hair. Cole's jaw clenched as he saw the outlines of guns under the taller men's shirts. He could no longer see the two men and knew Kate was still down the side street.

Cole wondered if these men were the ones she was worried about.

Not knowing what he was about to head into, he quickly dialed Officer Ander's number. It rang a couple times before his long-time friend answered.

"Hey, Cole."

"Where are you?" Cole grabbed the door handle and pushed open the door.

"I'm working a homicide downtown."

Cole let out a little sigh. "How quick can you get someone to the corner of Sixth and Fourth Street?"

"I'm finishing up my report now. I can meet you over there in twenty."

"Can you send someone?" Cole gripped his gun. "I think a woman might be in trouble and not sure I can take on three men at the same time."

Max spoke to someone in the background. "I'm radioing dispatch to send the closest unit. Don't go down there until you have backup. It will take me at least ten minutes to get to your location."

A scream echoed from Kate's location. "I need backup now." He swiped to end the call and placed the phone in his pocket. Cole ran down the sidewalk and turned the corner to see the woman on the ground, clutching her side. Kate was on her knees twenty feet away, her eyes shut tight. The man in dress pants had a gun pointed at her head.

Cole raised his Glock and aimed for the man's leg. He squeezed the trigger. The bullet whizzed out of the gun and hit the target perfectly. The man screamed and dropped to the ground, clutching his leg. Blood seeped out of the man's wound. His two men fell to the ground next to their boss and tried to help stop the bleeding. Kate slowly opened her eyes; she looked from the man on the ground holding his calf to Cole. She eyed him for a couple seconds before jumping up and running toward the back of the alleyway, and Cole cursed under his breath.

The man on the ground yelled for his men to kill Cole. Cole never took his gun off the three men. One man favored his right leg and limped when he took a step toward Cole. Neither of them had picked up the gun from the ground.

"Leave," the one without a limp shouted.

"How about you guys go, and we forget what happened? I've already radioed the cops, and they will be here any second."

The man on the floor grunted, "Fuck," as he gripped his hand around his bleeding leg.

"None of this is your concern," the man in the suit shirt shouted.

Cole slowly took another step to the side. He wanted to get to the woman in the back of the alley, hunched over a few cardboard boxes. He needed to get her attention so he could wave for her to leave.

"Here is what is going to happen: the police will be here in a few minutes, and you can explain why I found you with a gun to a woman's head." Cole's eyes never left the three men threatening his and Kate's life. In the distance, he could hear the faint sound of a cop car.

Hearing the sirens, the two men looked at each other then rushed back to their boss and helped him stand.

The man wearing the gray suit pants glared at Cole. "The cops won't do a thing."

Max had told Ian and him about how the police department had a few corrupt cops, and they've been working to clean up the department. "Well, the cop coming isn't on your payroll. He's a friend of mine." Cole smirked and motioned with his gun for them to leave.

The two bodyguards hunched down and helped their boss stand. "Don't think this is over. I will find you and make you wish we'd never met."

Cole never took his eyes off the three men until they turned the corner. Once they were gone, Cole rushed down the dirty alleyway to Kate's side. She had her hands pressed to the side of a man lying on the ground. The metallic smell of blood overpowered the scent of body odor and old food. He breathed out of his mouth to keep from gagging.

Years of medical training kicked in, Cole pressed his fingers to the man's wrist, he could faintly feel his pulse. Two cop cars came to a screeching halt at the entrance of the alleyway, Kate stiffened next to him as Max ran toward them.

"We need to get him to an ambulance."

"Please don't let him die," Kate begged.

ZOEY

"Ma'am, you need to move."

Zoey hadn't heard the paramedic come up behind her until he spoke, but it was the hand on her shoulder that startled her. She'd been watching Paul's chest rise with each breath and kept hoping he would make it until help came. Paul had helped her through the worst of living on the streets, and now he might die because of her.

The man Zoey had tried to shoot less than an hour ago continued to press his hand against Paul's wound and talk to the paramedics as they took over the scene. She'd moved to the side so the men and woman could work on him, but she still gripped his large calloused hand in hers. Zoey hadn't even realized she'd been crying until the wet tear hit her hand

and dripped onto Paul's. Maybe if she had stayed and not gone to the house, Paul wouldn't be in critical condition, and Al might still be alive.

Zoe looked over to the side of the alleyway and watched as an officer took pictures of the scene. She could tell them precisely who'd killed Al, but Zoey didn't know who to trust after Nixson's men had destroyed her home. Everything she'd ever owned had gone up in smoke, including the only picture she had of her mom. The fire marshal had tried to say it looked like she'd left a curling iron on, which was impossible. Zoey had never owned a curling iron, but they showed her pictures of one sitting on the burnt counter in her bathroom. Someone had planted the evidence, and the police had done nothing to figure out the truth, even though Zoey had told them her side.

"Kate, come stand over here."

She still couldn't believe the man she'd shot at earlier had saved her life. Knowing the paramedics needed to do their job, she squeezed Paul's hand one more time before standing.

"Thank you." The words didn't seem like enough. *But what do you say to the person who saved you from dying?*

"For what?"

"Saving me from being shot or hauled off to a torture chamber."

"Anyone would've done the same thing."

She looked from the paramedics to the man next to her. "No sane person would save someone who shot at them earlier."

"I'm sane." His lip turned up, and the cocky smile made him look even hotter than before.

"I need to leave." The police would start to ask questions, and she didn't know who to trust. Nixson would have someone watching the streets, so she needed to run. Every second she waited around was another second Eric could regroup and come after her.

"Do you trust me?"

"No."

"Good answer—you shouldn't trust anyone you just met, but you do owe me."

Zoey squared her shoulders, ready to take on the man who was trying to blackmail her into something. She was done letting people bully her. Zoey took another look at the man. He was wearing a navy-blue polo shirt that was tight around the muscles on his biceps. His short blond hair was a mess from running his hand through it, but she wanted to see his crystal blue eyes again when she told the man off.

"I don't owe anyone." The words came out louder than she'd expected, and everyone stopped what they were doing and looked at her.

"Okay, Kate, you don't owe me, but I want to help. How about after we talk to the police, me and you head to a restaurant for lunch?"

"I really need to go. I can't talk to the police, and no to food. No place will let me in. I know how bad I smell. It's enough to make me sick, but I have no food in my stomach to throw up."

"Stay."

She really didn't like the fact that the arrogant man told her to stay like an ordinary house dog, but her feet didn't move. Instead, she watched as the man walked over to another man barking orders. The sound of a groan had her tearing her eyes from the two men talking to the paramedics lifting Paul onto a gurney and wheeling him down the alley. She rushed to his side and gripped his hand. Paul's lips moved, and she placed her ear over them. "Be safe" were the last words Paul said before the paramedic pulled her away.

Her eyes watered as she watched them load him up into the ambulance and leave. She wanted to go along but knew it would be too dangerous. When a hand touched her shoulder, her heart sped up, but she stopped herself from swinging and trying to take the person out.

"Didn't mean to scare you."

Zoey shrugged. "I wasn't paying attention."

He didn't call her out on her blatant lie—it was more than not paying attention to everything going on around her. "Can I go now?"

"Normally, you would need to give a statement, but Officer Anders said we can come down tomorrow or he could come to my house."

"Just like that."

"Uh-huh. Now I don't know about you, but I'm starving and could use a good meal. It's been one of those days. You know what I'm talking about, when you wake up, head to work, and someone shoots at you."

"Are you blackmailing me into going to eat with you?"

"No. I want to help you."

"Why?"

"Honestly, I don't know. Earlier, I could've called it a day and started to work on the house, but my gut told me you need help, so I followed you. Once again, my gut was right."

Zoey was surprised by his honesty. She'd really expected him to make up some reason, but he'd had every chance so far to turn her in to the police. Hell, he said he was friends with the man in charge of the crime scene. "You listen to your gut a lot?"

"Yes, now do you want to leave and grab food or give Officer Anders your statement?"

She shook her head, walked over to her bag, and grabbed the only possessions she had left.

The man watched her every step as she walked back toward him. He nodded to the police officer. "Let's go eat. How does steak sound?" he asked while he held out his hand for her bag.

Instead of handing it over, she held it closer to her body.

Without saying anything, he dropped his arm and walked toward his shiny Range Rover parked a few spots down.

"How about you go grab me some fast food, and I wait here?"

He studied her with a calculating look in his eye. "It's been a long day for both of us. How does a shower sound? And then we can go eat wherever you want."

Zoey nibbled on her lip. *A shower...* She hadn't let her guard down and taken a shower in sixty-four days. It had been her last, because when she came out, half of her things had been stolen. Right then, she'd sworn she wouldn't let anyone do that to her again.

When she didn't answer him, he asked, "Would you feel safer if I gave you my phone and you could call anyone you wanted or 911?"

"Where can I take a shower?"

"My house, and before you say no, I promise not to kill you."

Zoey couldn't help but smile. "Isn't that something a serial killer might say?"

"Maybe. I could let you talk to my good friend." He let out a sigh. "I just want to help."

"Let's go." *I'll probably regret those words later, when I'm lying in a bathtub of ice with a missing organ.*

"Cole!" The officer's voice rang out from down the alley. "Hold up for a second."

"What's up, man?" Cole asked, stepping to her side and facing his friend.

The officer looked at Zoey. "I thought you might want to know they took your friend to University Hospital."

"Thank you."

"Any time. I'm sorry for your other friend. Don't forget you both owe me a statement tomorrow."

The officer said before turning back to the crime scene.

"Your name is Cole?"

They both turned and started toward the SUV. Over the last few months, she'd learned to ignore the looks of disgust from others, but it was harder today. *Is he judging me like everyone else?*

"Yep, are you going to tell me your real name, or do you want me to keep calling you Kate?"

"Zoey."

Cole opened the passenger side door of the SUV. "Zoey fits you so much better than Kate."

She shrugged. "Kate was the first name that popped into my mind, and I wasn't about to tell some stranger my real name." Zoey sank into the black leather seats.

"Well, Zoey, who has no last name, let's go find a shower." He shut the door before she could respond, but she wasn't sure what she would have said anyway. Cole had been helpful so far, but she wasn't ready to tell him her last name.

She watched as he rounded the car and climbed into the driver's seat. For the first time in months, Zoey felt safe, which was strange, since she barely knew the guy. "Probably should've asked earlier but where do you live?"

Cole snorted and pulled into traffic. "I'm not going to kill you. My house is in the Terrell Hills area."

"Terrell Hills is expensive. What were you doing in that rundown house earlier today, if you weren't coming for me?"

"My partner and I buy homes and flip them once we finish the remodel. I purchased the house you were in today from the Bexar County Courthouse. I expected maybe a few squatters, never someone to shoot at me."

"Sorry."

Zoey watched the road as Cole drove down the streets of San Antonio. Colorful tattoos covered his arms. Instead of making her look at him differently, the cartoon images on his forearm added to his sexy edge. She wanted to run her fingers over the designs and ask what had made him decide to add the art to his body, but she didn't want to be rude.

If she hadn't been so scared after Eric found her, she probably would've kept running and not gotten into his SUV. She hadn't figured out why Cole wanted to help her, but when he mentioned food, her stomach growled loudly.

"You don't have to keep apologizing. Now let's

talk about something else... If you could have anything to eat for dinner, what would it be?"

She let out a breath. Her favorite food was not the question she expected him to ask. She'd tried to not think about food because she hadn't even thought she would get to eat non-expired food again. "Steak with mashed potatoes—ohh, and a side of asparagus," she blurted out.

"No dessert?"

"Warm apple pie with ice cream." Her mouth watered as she thought about the last time she'd eaten a piece of pie. *Last Christmas...* Every year, she made a pie for Christmas dinner. Apple pie reminded Zoey of her mother, who'd passed away four years ago from breast cancer.

"Apple pie is one of my favorites."

The rest of the car ride, they spent asking each other what their favorite colors, tv shows, and sports teams were. Talking to Cole was easy, and for the first time in months, she felt satisfied with her decision. Zoey relaxed back into the comfy leather seat. She felt safer than she had in a long time. *How long will it last, though?*

His house was beautiful. It had a perfectly manicured lawn with a splash of color from yellow flowers around the front walkway. Not only was the yard perfect, but when they walked inside, his house was nothing like a bachelor pad. Everything had a place. The furniture matched and wasn't the usual black leather couch or single chair guys have in their bachelor pad. She'd immediately felt out of place—his house was clean, and she stank like yogurt left out in the sun for days.

"Cole, you can take me back to the shelter. I'm sorry I put you through all this today."

Instead of replying, he placed his hand on her lower back and moved her down the hallway. They passed two closed doors, which she assumed led to bedrooms, before leaving the entryway. She saw a large open concept kitchen. Cooking was never her forte, but she might try if she had a kitchen like that.

Cole cleared his throat and opened a door on the left. "This is the guest bedroom, and it has a shower. I will go grab you a pair of shorts and a T-shirt and set them on the bed while you shower. They will be a little big on you, but we can put your clothes in the washer or order some new ones in."

Tears pricked at the side of Zoey's eyes. Paul and Al had tried to help her, but this was more than anyone had done. "Thank you." Once again, the words didn't seem good enough to convey how she felt. She walked into the bedroom and straight for the shower. She couldn't wait to feel the warm water run down her body.

Zoey stopped and looked in the bathroom mirror. Her hair was so dirty, it seemed dark brown rather than light blond. Grime covered her pale skin. Not wanting to look at her reflection any longer, she turned and stripped off her clothes. Knowing a washer wouldn't get the smell and filth out of her clothes, she quickly put them in the bathroom trash and tied the bag in a knot. She turned on the shower and stood under the warm water.

The dirt running off her body turned the shower floor brown, but she couldn't analyze her feeling about how gross she was as fresh water ran over her body. Thirty minutes later, the water was still warm, but she knew it was time to get out and face the man who helped her today. Turning the knobs, she stopped the water, then she grabbed a soft-blue towel off the rack.

Opening the drawers, she looked for a brush to comb her hair. She couldn't help letting out the sigh when she saw the unopened toothbrush and comb. It felt like winning the lottery. After her time on the streets, she appreciated the little things way more than she had before.

After brushing her hair and teeth, Zoey slowly

opened the bathroom door to find a pair of athletic shorts and a T-shirt on the bed. The clean clothes were enormous on her emaciated frame.

Cole seemed like a good guy, but she'd also thought her old boss was a good guy in the beginning, until she'd returned to the office late one night after forgetting her cell phone and saw someone being tortured.

As Zoey walked back down the hall toward the kitchen, she heard Cole's voice. " I need more information out of her before I can call him ."

Her feet stumbled. *Seems he might not be the good guy...* And she had nowhere to run.

COLE

Cole pulled two steaks out of the refrigerator and sighed tiredly. The day had been filled with more excitement than he'd had in a while. Bella's rescue had provided a rush of adrenaline he had been missing since his time in the military. Nevertheless, something about Zoey made him want to throw caution to the wind and do whatever was necessary to protect her. He snorted to himself. They'd just met, and he would do anything to help her. He wanted to know everything about her. In the car ride to the house, he'd said they were playing a game to break the tension in the car by saying things they liked. That wasn't entirely true, though. He wanted to know everything about her, and he'd used the game to find out her favorite things. Purple was her favorite color, and she liked daisies instead of roses.

His phone vibrated on the counter, and he let out another sigh as Ian's name flashed across the screen. Cole knew he should've called Ian back a while ago to let him know everything was okay, but Cole wanted to spend every second he had talking to the wildcat. His mind wandered back to the fact that she was stripping down in his shower. His dick stirred as he thought about the water running over the swell of her breasts.

Maybe I can ignore Ian for another day. The phone started to vibrate again. Cole knew Ian and Bella would be on the first flight back, and Cole wanted them to spend time together. They deserved every minute of their vacation, and he wasn't going to be the one to stop it.

"Why aren't you enjoying your time away with your fiancée?" he asked as he preheated the oven for the potatoes.

Ian huffed on the other side of the phone. "Dude, you can't tell me you were shot at and going after the person who pulled the trigger. What did you expect me to do? Wait for the medical examiner to call?"

"I'm an ex-Navy SEAL. I think I can handle one

wildcat taking a shot at me. Now a mob of three gangsters were a little more challenging."

"What?" Ian yelled.

Cole punched holes in the potatoes with a fork before throwing them in the oven. "Everything is under control. I'm at my house, and no bullet holes." Cole snickered.

"We're heading back first thing in the morning," Ian said.

"No, I have everything under control, and if—and I mean if—I need you, I promise you will be my first call. Zoey is already on edge enough. I don't need you and Bella coming and making things even more complicated." Really, he wanted her to himself and wasn't ready to share her with his friends quite yet.

Ian didn't reply immediately. "Fine, but you know I'm here for you. Besides Bella, you're all the family I have."

Even though Cole had two other blood brothers he didn't speak to, Ian felt like the only family he had. When Bella was in trouble, Cole did everything to help, including calling his oldest brother and asking for help. He hadn't talked to Bryson in years, and now he owed him a favor. He would do the same thing again if it meant keeping Ian and Bella safe.

"If I need anything, you will be the first call I

make. Until then, enjoy your time with Bella and don't worry about me. I have everything under control." *Except my dick.* He didn't plan to tell his friend about that, though.

"Fine, but call Tex. This girl seems like she is in trouble. You know he would help you in a heartbeat. Hell, he'll be pissed if he finds out you didn't call for help."

"I need more information out of her before I can call him." He heard a gasp behind him before he finished his words. Those words wouldn't sound good if taken out of context. "I gotta go. I will call you if I need anything." Cole swiped end on the phone and turned to see Zoey staring daggers his way.

He loved her spunk. She hadn't given up, even though he could only imagine how unfair the world had been to her. Cole didn't know how long she had been on the street, but he had a feeling it hadn't been long. She wasn't jagged like others he had seen on the road. Zoey had a layer of innocence, and he wanted her to keep that and not let her see how fucked up the world really is.

"It's not what you think."

She placed her hands on her hips and narrowed her eyes further. "Really? To me, it sounded like you were going to get information out of me and give it to someone. I thought you might be one of the good guys, and here you are—working an angle."

Cole pulled out a chair and pointed. "Sit." When she didn't move, he continued. "I will tell you everything. Have a seat while I finish making dinner."

Zoey frowned. "The only reason I'm staying is because I want a piece of that bread." She walked over and sat at the counter. She had combed her long blond hair, and Cole liked the idea of her wearing his clothes. It made him feel like he'd helped a little in making her more comfortable.

He cut off a couple pieces of bread and poured olive oil into to a dish with minced garlic, so she could snack on something as he cooked her food. Her tongue peeked out and ran across her dry lips as he placed the bread in front of her. When she didn't pick it up, he told her to eat while he worked.

She let out a moan and closed her eyes as she popped a piece of bread into her mouth. Cole watched as she ate. It was the most erotic thing he had seen, which was strange because they were both wearing clothes. He shook his head to get his thoughts and body under control. "You didn't hear my whole conversation."

She rolled her eyes at him.

"Let me start from the beginning. Earlier, I told you my partner and I flip homes. The house you were in earlier is our next project. What you don't know is Ian and I have been friends longer than our flipping business. We met years ago in BUD/S." When she gave him a puzzled look he continued. "Basic Underwater Demolition SEAL school."

"As in a Navy SEAL?"

"Yes, I was a Navy SEAL. A few years back, I was medically discharged, but that's a story for another time." He closed his eyes and tried not to think about being captured and tortured for days in North Korea. If it weren't for their friend Tex, Cole and Ian would have died. "Ian called when I left the house earlier today, and I told him briefly what happened."

"You mean that I shot at you?"

Cole's lip turned up. "Yes, and I told him it looked like you needed help, so I was going to help you. I hadn't called him back, so he was worried about me. That was him on the phone. We have contacts in the government who can help you. He wanted to know if I used them."

Zoey closed her eyes for a second. "No, I've already put you through enough. I got myself into this. Now I need to get myself out."

"Sometimes, we need help getting out of trouble

and have to ask for help or take it when it is offered. Why don't you want me to help you get out of this or whatever is going on?"

Cole finished putting salt and pepper on the steaks before putting them in the frying pan. He wanted Zoey to think about his question and not give him the first answer that came to mind.

"I'm not used to asking for help or accepting it. My mother did everything to raise me, and nobody helped. Now all I've done in the last three months is take, and look where that got Paul—stabbed! And Al is dead. Now if I bring you in, I might get you killed. I'm not even sure why I came here."

"Eight years ago, I was on SEAL Team Five. We were on a mission in North Korea to bring back information on a missing SEAL team the CIA had uncovered. The information was false, according to a CIA mole in North Korea. When our team arrived to save the missing SEAL team, the North Koreans ambushed us. They tortured my team for five days. It had felt like a year. Ian and I were the only two to survive the torture. Later, information came out that the CIA mole had flipped sides and had been helping North Korea. Do you think I got out on my own?" Cole turned and flipped the steaks to the other side and pulled out the potatoes. He considered locking

Zoey in his panic room while he hunted down the men after her. It wasn't logical, but nothing he did seemed to be logical today.

"I don't know where to start."

"How about with why the men are after you?"

She shook her head.

Cole let a sigh. "How about we start simple? What's your last name?"

She narrowed her eyes at him.

"My last name is Walker. Now let me know yours, and we can see if anyone has put a bounty out on you. Those men I met in the alley earlier didn't seem like very nice men and normally not ones I see doing the dirty work."

He pushed the plate with steak, potatoes, and salad toward her. Cole wished he had apple pie in the fridge to make her happy, but he wasn't much of a sweets person and didn't have anything for dessert. He planned to change that tomorrow.

"You know how to find things on the dark web?" she asked.

Her question was another stall tactic. Cole didn't care how long they would need to talk for her to trust him with her personal information. "No, but I know a guy."

"You know a guy?" Her laughter filled the

kitchen. "That sounds like something a mobster would say."

"My guy has nothing to do with the mob. He is a well-respected military veteran. I promise I won't use any of the information he finds against you. I just want to help."

"That's what my friend said when she got me the job with them." Zoey took a bite of steak, and when she finished chewing, she added, "Thomas."

"Is that your last name or who you worked for?"

Zoey slowly took another bite of her food. Cole didn't care she was taking her time answering him and analyzing every word before it came out of her mouth. She didn't trust him, and that hurt a little, but he didn't push. He waited, knowing if he demanded answers, she would stop talking. That was the last thing he wanted.

"My last name." She pointed to the food. "This is really good. I know I've only eaten garbage for the past three months, but this steak is perfect."

Cole tucked away that bit of information she hadn't realized she'd let slip. He'd been right when he assumed she'd been homeless for about three months. Now he had to get her to trust him enough to tell him what she was running from.

"Can I have my friend look to see if he can find

anything?" Cole knew he was pushing, but he wanted Zoey safe, and Tex would get him one-step closer to finding out what is going on. "I will let you listen to the phone call."

"Why do you think this Tex guy can help?"

"Tex can find anything."

"He sounds like a hacker."

Cole let out a sigh. "Honestly, some of the things he does is probably illegal, but he's effective. Tex knows people high up in the military and can get things done quicker than I've ever seen. If it weren't for him, I would be dead. I owe him my life, and still every time I need something, he is there for me and asks nothing in return. He hates to be thanked."

"I don't want to bother him. He sounds busy, and I got myself into trouble."

"We all do something we wish we could change. Tex isn't going to judge you. Do you want to hear what he has to say?"

When she nodded, he pulled out his cell and clicked Tex's name.

The phone rang three times before he answered. "Hello?" Tex said in his familiar Southern accent.

"Hey, Tex, it's Cole." He tapped the speaker button on his phone so Zoey could hear the conversation. "I have my friend Zoey Thomas on speaker with me."

"Hello, darlin'."

"Hi."

"Are Ian and Bella okay?" Tex asked quickly.

Zoey's eyes went to him, asking what he was talking about. He would tell her about Bella later. First, he needed Tex to start working on Zoey's issue. "Bella and Ian are fine and off in a cabin, celebrating their engagement."

"They deserve happiness after what they went through. I'm glad you called, but I have a feeling y'all didn't call to talk."

Cole spent the next five minutes telling Tex about the house he'd bought and how he'd found Zoey. She hadn't said a word since hi. Cole hoped she would tell Tex something so they could get the people off her back.

"Zoey, you need to let Cole take you to the shooting range."

He didn't wait for Zoey to reply. "Already planning on it tomorrow and then to the gun store."

"From the sounds of it, you have some bad people after you, Zoey. Do you know what they want?"

"Yes."

He waited for her to elaborate. "We need more than a yes."

"I witnessed my boss kill someone."

Tex let out a whistle. "Let's start with your boss's name."

"Clyde Walker."

Of all the names he'd expected to come out of her mouth, Clyde's was not one of them. That made things much trickier.

"You're telling me you watched Clyde kill someone?" Cole asked.

"Yes."

Tex cleared his throat on the other side. "Cole, I have to ask if you want me to take care of this. Don't get me wrong—I've wanted to take him down for years."

Zoey gave Cole a strange look, and he rubbed his hand down his face. "Yes, find out as much information on my uncle as possible. It's time I take down my family."

ZOEY

Zoey pushed her roller through the light-gray paint before running it down the wall in the master bedroom of Cole's flip. She'd spent the last week helping him work on the house, and in return, she had food and a place to stay until they figured out what to do about Clyde, Cole's uncle. When he'd first told her his last name, she hadn't thought much about it. Walker was a common last name. She hadn't expected her arch enemy to be related to Cole.

The day after, they spent most of the day downtown at the station, talking to Officer Anders. Even though he didn't flat out say Clyde had people on his payroll, he hinted at it, and he was working to see what he could do. Officer Anders wanted to stop the corruption at the police department.

He had ordered her enough clothes off Amazon to last her three months without changing. Each day when they arrived back at the house, another package sat on the doorstep. He promised no more, but she had a feeling he wouldn't stop. They argued about the amount he bought, but he refused to return them. Zoey planned to donate some clothes once she got back on her feet.

"You want to take a break and come with me to the hardware store?" Cole asked as he crossed his arms.

"No, I'm almost done with this room," Zoey replied as she dipped her roller in paint.

"The wall will be here when we get back," Cole joked.

"I know." Ian had called Cole the night before. He and Bella were coming back tomorrow, and Zoey wanted them to be excited with how much was done on the house. She looked around the master bedroom, the same room where she'd crouched and hidden, and smiled. The house had changed so much in a short time. While Cole waited for the flooring for the bedroom to come in, he worked on gutting the bathroom. He'd shown her his mock-up of what he planned to do. She couldn't wait to see the finished project. The first day, they'd cleared out the garbage lying around the house and scrubbed the walls with warm soap to remove the poop. They couldn't save all the walls; some of the area in the main living room needed to be ripped out. Zoey's arms ached from the physical labor. Typing on her computer for years hadn't built any arm muscles. "I want to finish this wall."

Cole grabbed the other roller on the floor and dipped it in the paint. "I'll help you finish. The hardware store wasn't the only place I wanted to stop."

He started on the opposite corner of the wall. His biceps stretched his black T-shirt as he rolled the paint. Zoey had to close her mouth because she was sure she was drooling. He'd taken his shirt off the other day while they were working on cleaning up the yard. She almost fainted, and it wasn't from the heat. Over the past week, she had learned his routine: six-o'clock workout followed by healthy breakfast, read the paper, then wake her up.

"Where else are we going?" Zoey eyed him carefully.

Cole liked to give her things or take her to

expensive places. They had been tiptoeing around their attraction. Each night, it got harder as they would lay on the couch and watch TV. Last night, he'd run his hand along her leg, and she'd almost jumped him. Zoey didn't know how much longer she would last without touching him.

"It's a surprise."

"I'm already in debt to you enough, Cole. I can't afford these surprises. Not sure if I will ever be able to pay you back."

He dropped his roller, and the metal handle clattered against the hard floor. He was in front of her within seconds, standing close—really close. She could smell his woodsy scent, and his hand running down her arm was enough for her body to lean into him.

"You don't owe me anything," he growled. "Furthermore, where I'm taking you is free." Cole leaned in and ran his thumb across her cheek.

She closed her eyes and took a couple deep breaths, getting her body back under control.

He continued, "You had a smidge of paint on your face."

Zoey contemplated smearing more paint on her face to have his hands on her. Instead, she stepped back and took a couple deep breaths. Cole's pupils were dilated; she wasn't the only affected by the gesture.

An hour later, she was climbing into Cole's SUV. Over the past week, she had talked with Tex a few times. Even though they wanted to help, she wasn't ready to tell them everything. Cole said Tex was excellent, and if he was, he would figure out what she'd done. The thumb drive was in her pocket. She hadn't said a word about it yet. When she talked with Tex and Cole, she'd only said she'd seen what her boss did. She wasn't ready to give up her only leverage. Cole could change his mind at any second and decide to help his uncle. While it was getting harder to keep the secret about the thumb drive, she knew it wasn't right what she was doing.

Zoey squeezed the thumb drive. "Can you please tell me where we are going?" The possibility of him driving her to meet his uncle popped into her mind first. "Have I not told you I don't like surprises?" She wasn't used to them. Her mother didn't have much money when she was growing up, so there were never gifts from the store or nice restaurants. It might not have been any kid's dream, but Zoey wouldn't change her childhood. She'd had her mom, and that was all she'd needed.

Cole reached over and grasped her thigh; it sent

an electric shock through her body. She squeezed her legs together to relieve some tension in her body.

"We are going to visit a friend."

Her heart sank. The only friend she could think of was his friend. Zoey didn't have any. She used to have one, and she was the reason Zoey was on the run.

"Woo, you tensed. Who do you think we are going to see?"

She let out a long sigh. "I'm not sure, but I don't have any friends, so I assume you are taking me to meet one of yours."

"That's what you really think? That I would protect you for a week and then one day take you to meet my uncle? I really thought you were starting to trust me." Cole ran his hand over his face and let out an aggravated breath. "We're going to meet Paul."

"Shit. I'm sorry. I don't know why I keep feeling like the other grenade is going to drop and blow up my life even more."

"Ball."

Zoey barked out a laugh. "It feels more like waiting for a grenade, not a ball, and I've had a fucked-up year. If I want to change the saying, I can.

Truly, I'm sorry about doubting you. There is no reason I should, but it creeps back into my mind. He's your uncle, and I'm just some woman you found in your house who shot at you. Please don't give up on me. I need more time."

The light turned red, and Cole stopped. "I've known for years my family is fucked up, and that is the reason I chose to join the Navy and walk away." His fingers turned white as he gripped the steering wheel. "If I would've stayed back and done something when I was younger, you wouldn't be running for your life."

A couple nights ago, he'd told her about his family and life growing up. Cole came from an extremely wealthy family. She'd wanted to cry when he explained how his mother never cared if he was home. His nanny had been more of a mother to him than his own.

"You have no reason to apologize for your family." She gripped the thumb drive in her pocket. "Tonight can we call Tex? I have more to talk about."

Cole glanced at her. "What else do you have?"

"It might work to help take down your uncle. If I give you what I have on him, I won't have anything left for him to keep me alive." After the last meeting in the alleyway, she wasn't so sure he cared if she was alive or dead as long as his info didn't get out. She'd planned to make a copy and put it in a safe deposit box, but she was scared it would be traced. Her job in Houston working for the Black brothers had been fantastic. Jared could be an ass most of the time, but he would never have put a hit out on her.

She'd never imagined anyone would put a hit out on her life, but Tex had told Cole he'd found one on the dark web. For a hundred thousand dollars, they would take her alive or dead, as long as they had proof she'd been killed. Tex had promised he was working to trace the hit back to Clyde—they needed evidence he'd put out the hit. At the moment, the hit didn't trace back to Clyde; it led to a shell company. She was told this was the way to cover up who'd ordered the hit.

Cole frowned as he pulled up in front of an apartment complex. The building was old but kept up, and a few flowers had been planted in the front. "We can make a copy of whatever you have so you still have one."

"Really?" She rested her head against the headrest. "You are too good to me, Cole. I don't know how I will ever repay you."

"Go on a date with me." Cole's statement left no room for error.

Zoey didn't know if he was doing it because he liked her or because he wanted more information. She needed to stop looking at him as the bad guy—he'd done nothing but try to help her from day one. "We've been hanging out together every day for the last week. I think we've been on a few dates."

Cole took her hand. The same electrical current she'd felt the first time he touched her went through her body. "Let's get dressed up and go out to a nice restaurant and catch a movie."

"Okay."

He ran his hand down her face and sent chills through her body. "Now that is solved, let me walk you to Paul's apartment while I go and run errands."

"You're not staying?"

"I thought you would want some time with your friend. He's a good guy, and I trust him."

Zoey let out a snort. "You mean Tex ran a background on him."

Cole didn't deny or confirm her suspicions; he jumped out of the SUV and came around to her side. She was used to it. He liked opening the door for her even though she always said it wasn't necessary.

When he opened the door, she climbed out, wrapped her arms around him, and placed her lips to his.

When she went to pull back, he tightened his hold and deepened the kiss. His tongue swiped against her lips, and she opened, letting him in. Her body felt like it was melting into his. Cole released his grip and pressed his forehead to hers. "If Paul hadn't seen us drive up, I would take you back home and spend hours worshiping your body."

Looking around, she quickly saw the curtain drop, and her face heated up. Cole leaned in and kissed her nose. "Let's go see Paul."

"You could've told me he was watching."

"I like this shade of pink on you." He teased.

Zoey lightly punched his shoulder as he wrapped his arm around her and directed her toward the first-floor apartment. The door swung open before Cole even had time to knock. Paul stood in the doorway, looking much better than he had when she'd last seen him. He was clean-shaven and wearing new clothes. Zoey hadn't asked Cole how he'd gotten Paul an apartment, but she knew Cole had something to do with it. The older man stepped out and squeezed her with one arm. The other hand rested on a cane.

"I'm happy you're alive," he whispered into Zoey's ear.

She pulled back. "Me too."

Paul stuck out his hand to Cole. "And you, I don't know how I will ever repay you for this."

Cole shifted from foot to foot. "I didn't do anything but find a few veterans benefits."

"It takes years to get moved through the list. I don't know who you know, but it has to be someone powerful."

"It's the least I can do to repay you for looking out for Zoey. I'm going to go run some errands while you guys talk. You have that gun, right?"

Paul nodded.

Cole kissed her on the cheek and left before she was able to ask about a gun. He had done so much without her asking. She'd been worried about Paul and how he was going to handle the streets with his wound. Every time she asked Cole, he said it was being taken care of and that she could see him soon.

Paul moved her through the small apartment. The place was barely decorated, filled only with the necessities—a couch, chair, tv, and table. There were no pictures on the walls, no knickknacks, or even a splash of color. Zoey made a note that when she had money and could work again, she would do whatever it took to help make Paul's place a home.

Over the next hour, Paul told her how Cole's friend, whom she assumed was Tex, had gotten him into veteran supportive housing. She felt guilty for not having known he was a veteran. He told her about his time in the military, and she couldn't believe he was part of Delta Force. His story was inspirational and sad. When he talked about the people he'd saved, his face lit up. When she asked if he had a family, a shadow fell over his face.

"I lived for my job and each mission. When I met Sarah, we were young, and she got pregnant. She wanted to stay at home and raise our son, but I wanted to save the world. The more deployments I took, the more we grew apart." Paul wiped his eyes. "One day, when I came back, they were gone, and I threw myself into the next mission and the next. Until one day, I was so angry at the world for what people had done. When I was medically discharged, I had nothing. My son hates me for leaving his mother. Sarah remarried, and my son considers him more a dad than me."

"Someday he will see what a good guy you are."

Paul rocked back in his chair. "I can't change what I did in the past, but I can change how I act in the future. Now that boy you found is a good one. He will protect you and keep you safe. Not sure how, but he has contacts deep inside the government."

"He is a goo—"

The sound of squealing tires cut her off, and before she knew what was going on, Paul threw her to the ground and covered her with his body. The sound of glass breaking echoed through the room. They'd found her.

COLE

"How's the new roommate working out?" Ian asked Cole as he took a sip of beer. On his way to the store, Ian had called to tell him they'd made it in a day earlier. Instead of meeting at the house, they were stopping to have a beer together. Cole figured it would give Zoey more time with Paul.

"Good."

"Have you talked to your dad or uncle and tried to get information?"

"No." Cole shrugged. "I gave Tex full authorization to tear into my family. He's wanted to do it for years, and I think he already did a couple years back when he told me I should watch out for them. Back then, I still wanted nothing to do with them."

"Your brother helped us out the other day. Maybe he isn't as bad as you think."

Cole knew that wasn't the case. His brother had only helped him out because now Cole owed him one. His grandfather had built a billion-dollar empire on being owed favors, and that was how his family worked. In two days, he would need to face his family, and he didn't know how Zoey would react to him going to see them. The idea of not telling her had crossed his mind, but that wouldn't be fair to her and would break what little trust she had if she found out. "Well, I will find out on Sunday what he really wants." Cole rolled his neck, trying to release the tension. "Eighteen years hasn't been long enough."

"I'm not saying you should break out the champagne and open yourself up. Go see what they want and get the answers you need," Ian continued. "They're family Cole."

"One thing the Navy taught me is family isn't always blood, but I'm going to try to get information to help Zoey. It's my family after her—why not go to the source? I'm hoping Tex will have more information for me before I go."

"Are you taking Zoey with?"

"I don't know. I'm scared for her to stay alone."

"Wolf's wife, Caroline, is coming to town on Sunday. She'll be here all next week for a science thing. She's coming over Sunday for dinner. Zoey can come hang out with Bella and Caroline if she wants."

"I appreciate you offering for her to come over. I still have to tell her about me heading to Dallas on Sunday. Bryson already sent me notification a private plane would be waiting for me. I'm tempted to ask Tex for a tracking device for me like he's given Caroline. Tex said he was going to monitor the plane, but I'm not sure where it might go."

"I'm not sure if it's a good idea you going by yourself," Ian noted matter-of-factly.

Cole shrugged and ran his hand through his hair. "Tex will call you if something goes wrong. I can't just sit back and wait for someone to make a move on Zoey."

"What does she have on your uncle?"

"You know how they've been looking for Senator Cramer? Well, Zoey watched my uncle kill him, and she said she knows he has another set of books."

Ian let out a whistle. "No wonder he put a hit on her head."

"Yeah."

The two men sipped their beers and sat in silence

for a beat. "Earlier today, she admitted she has proof but is scared to show me."

Ian shook his head. "What kind of proof?"

"No clue," Cole spat, harsher than he'd meant. Ian didn't comment on the outburst, so he continued. "She's worried I might take the info and turn her over. She doesn't trust me."

"Hmm."

"Really? That's all you have to say?"

"Give her time. You've known her a week. Tell her about seeing your brothers. The sooner, the better, because if you wait too long, she will think you're hiding something."

"Okay, enough about me and my troubles. How was your vacation? Did you guys enjoy your time away?"

"It was amazing, but it's nice to be back to the house, and we are ready to start on it tomorrow," Ian said.

"Zoey is almost done with painting the master bedroom. The tile for the bathroom should be in this week. Next week, I plan to start working on the kitchen."

"You helped me a lot when Bella was being bothered," Ian commented.

"It was nothing."

Ian narrowed his eyes. "Everything you did meant a lot to Bella and I. We are a team, so don't worry about the house. Bella and I got everything under control."

"I will let you know if I need anything. Zoey and I plan on being at the property tomorrow morning. Maybe a little late. I plan to take her out tonight. We've spent every night watching movies, but I wanted to do something different."

Ian's face lit up. "What are you planning?"

"I'm taking her out to eat and then for a walk along the River Walk." Cole looked down at his watch, suddenly realizing how much time had passed. He and Ian said their goodbyes, then he walked to the door and quickly made it to his car. He and Zoey were going on their first date, but it felt like they'd started dating when they first met. Zoey meant a lot to him, and he wanted to do everything in his power to make sure she was okay. That meant meeting with his family, soon.

The pub Ian and Cole had stopped at wasn't far from Paul's apartment. Tex had worked his magic to get Paul into housing for disabled vets. Two nights ago, Paul had called and thanked him for everything, but all Cole had done was ask for Tex's help. One thing Cole knew was not to thank Tex. He would repay him with a prank, and Cole already had enough going on.

Three cops roared passed Cole as he drove to Paul's house. His gut turned as an ambulance raced by. Cole pressed down on his gas pedal and called Zoey's number. It went to voicemail. He quickly called Paul, but it also went straight to voicemail. The police could be heading anywhere, but Cole had a feeling that wasn't the case. He didn't know what he was about to walk into, and he might need Ian's help.

Ian answered on the first ring. "Miss me already?"

"I was just passed by the cops and an ambulance. Zoey and Paul aren't answering."

"On my way."

The tires to Cole's SUV squealed as he turned the corner into the parking lot of Paul's complex. His worst fear had come true. Paramedics were working on someone outside Paul's apartment. He slammed his breaks and threw open the door. Yellow tape marked off the area, but Cole ran through it toward the paramedics.

"You can't be over here, sir."

Cole ignored the officer and ran faster toward the paramedics.

An officer grabbed him around the waist and yanked him back. "This is a crime scene, sir, you need to step behind the yellow tape."

With a quick turn, he ducked out of the officer's grip, and when he turned, he saw Zoey running down the sidewalk toward him. He let out a breath for the first time, stepping to the side. He ran toward her and threw his arms around her.

She was shaking, and her tears dripped onto his shoulder. "It's okay."

"Are you okay?" Cole stepped back and ran his hands down her arms.

"I didn't get hurt, but Paul's wound reopened when he covered me."

He pulled her closer while he looked back at the apartment. Cops walked around the front window. Glass covered the front flowers and sidewalk. "What happened?"

"We were talking about Paul's family when we heard tires squeal, and Paul threw himself over me. The next thing I know, the window shattered, and a large brick crashed through the front window."

As Cole led Zoey away from the scene. The day was already warm, although not as humid as a typical summer day in Texas. Ian pulled in next to his SUV, jumped out of his truck, and rushed to Cole's side.

"You must be Zoey." Ian held out his hand.

Zoey's brows came down in confusion. "Yes. Who are you? You don't sound like Tex."

Ian burst out laughing. "I'm lucky if I can even turn on my computer, much less hack a satellite or whatever he hacks. I'm Ian."

Cole watched as his friend pulled Zoey in for a one-armed hug because Cole still hadn't let her other arm go. He needed to touch her.

Someone followed us. That was the only explanation. *Who knows what they'll come at her with next time?* "I think you've hugged long enough," Cole grumbled.

"Cole," Zoey said as she quickly stepped back and smiled at him. "Are you really being jealous of your friend who is happily engaged?"

"Maybe we should take a look at the damage," Cole said, completely ignoring Zoey's question.

Ian smiled at him, knowing exactly what his friend did. "We'll need to get some boards to close up the window."

The three of them walked over to the front of the apartment, making sure to stay to the side so they wouldn't contaminate the crime scene. One detective was taking pictures inside the apartment while another was working outside.

"They aren't going to stop until they have me." Zoey let out a shaky breath. "I need to find a different place to stay or leave town."

"Everything will be okay. We just need a little more time. I'll call my friend in Fort Lauderdale and have them send a bodyguard out to watch over Paul once he's released."

"Don't worry about boarding the window," Ian added. "I can take care of it. You both have other things to figure out, and this will help me repay you for staying and cleaning up Bella's house after she was attacked. I know the only thing you want to do right now is take Zoey to your house and make sure she's okay."

"Hello. I'm right here," Zoey said, annoyance in her voice.

"We know you are here, and I'm not letting you run. Ian feels like he owes me for being a friend," Cole said.

"You go have a good night. I'm going to talk to the police and see when I can board up the place. Do you want me to run by the hospital and check on Paul?"

"Yes, please."

Ian walked with them back to the SUV. Cole leaned in and gave his friend a hug, then Ian pulled Zoey into another hug.

"It was great meeting you, Zoey. I wish it was under better circumstances. Bella can't wait to meet the woman who shot at Cole."

"Can we not talk about that?" Zoey asked, covering her face. "That wasn't my best moment."

"I don't think you are ever going to live that down. I wanted to head out to the range tomorrow. Do you and Bella want to go before we head over to the house?"

They had gone a couple times, and she was getting better each time. His uncle was getting desperate or worried. It would only be a matter of time before he found out Cole was helping her.

He wanted to put his fist through a wall. Every morning Tex didn't have an answer and the count-down to meeting his family neared, Cole ran an extra mile. He was up to ten miles, and it did nothing to control his anger at the situation.

His family ruining people's lives was the reason he'd distanced himself years ago. They were all the scum of the earth. No matter how much time passed, deep down, he knew they were the same. Now Cole wanted to take them down.

"Tomorrow is good."

"See you tomorrow."

"Hey, Cole, If you need anything else, call."

Years ago, Cole learned family wasn't always blood, and today, that showed. Ian would do anything for him, and Cole would do the same for his friend. Cole waved over his shoulder. "Thanks!"

Zoey squeezed his hand. "Your friend is pretty cool."

"I know."

"Okay, let's get home so I can show you what I have," she told him as she climbed into the car.

Cole held the door open for a second. "I'm glad you took a shot at me."

"Stop making fun of me."

He leaned in and lightly brushed his lips against hers. "I'm not. I would never make fun of you. I really like being around you."

Cole kissed the tip of her nose before shutting the door and heading to the other side and getting in. "Let's head home."

"Home," Zoey repeated.

Cole hoped what she had was enough to bring down his uncle, because after today, Cole wouldn't stop until his uncle was behind bars or six feet under.

On the car ride back to his house, they talked about cooking in for the night and going out tomorrow. Neither of them was in the mood for a night out. When they pulled up to the house, Cole's anger rose. Zoey tensed next to him.

"Who is that?"

A man his height but with a bigger build leaned against a Bugatti in his driveway. Cole knew that he had the same piercing blue eyes under his sunglasses as he did. "My brother."

ZOEY

Zoey gripped the door tightly. She didn't know what to expect. Cole reached over and grabbed a gun out of the glove box. Zoey wanted to tell him to put the car in reverse and run for the state lines rather than get into a shootout with his own brother. Then another man stepped out of the expensive car.

"Fuckers," Cole mumbled under his breath as he grabbed the clip to go along with the black gun. Zoey didn't know what kind it was; it looked similar to the one she'd tried to shoot, but larger and more deadly. Zoey laughed at herself for a second. *All guns are dangerous.*

Cole leaned over and pressed his lips to hers. He pulled away more quickly than she would have liked. The sun was setting over the house, making it harder to see the men's facial expressions. Cole needed backup. She wouldn't let him face these two men alone.

"Call Ian, or let's leave."

Cole smiled. "They won't hurt me."

"Then why the gun?"

He didn't reply as he climbed out of the SUV and walked toward his brothers. Over the past week, he had filled her in on bits and pieces about his family. Growing up, his brothers were inseparable, but he hadn't told her what had made them grow apart. She knew he'd left because of his dad. Maybe his brothers held that against him.

Zoey quickly looked around the car for something that might help. She had a good feeling whatever he was about to walk into was because of her. Making a quick decision, she grabbed the paint can from the back seat and jumped out of the car. It wasn't the best weapon, but it might be useful.

Cole's head whipped around when he heard the car door slam. "Stay in the car, Zoey."

Zoey's heart was beating a mile a minute. For a split second, she considered getting back in the car. Instead, she marched up the driveway and stood next to Cole. "Are you going to introduce me?"

He clenched his jaw and stared at his brothers.

They all looked so much alike, except the one on the right had a beard. She assumed it was his older brother. He had a few lines under his eyes and was the tallest. Next to him stood an equally handsome man with laugh lines. He didn't seem to be as angry as the older one.

"I told you to stay in the car, Zoey," Cole gritted out.

"And I choose to ignore your demand. Last time I checked, I wasn't five. Now, are you going to invite them in and figure out why they are here, or are we going to stand in the driveway with a gun out and let old Mrs. Smith watch the whole thing go down?"

It took a second for the words to sink in before Cole slipped his gun into his waistband and turned to wave at his next-door neighbor. The old lady narrowed her eyes but waved back. "She needs to learn to mind her own business," Cole huffed.

The oldest of the brothers stuck out his hand. "I like you. I'm Bryson, and this is Nathan, since Cole is so rude." Bryson gave her a panty-dropping smile. When she went to reach for his hand, Cole batted it away.

"Let's go inside and you can tell me why you are here. I'm still not convinced you're here to help."

Lord. These three men are deadly hot. Zoey was going to need to pick her jaw up off the ground as she walked behind the brothers. Zoey watched them all carefully. Bryson seemed tired, but Cole was tense, ready to take his brothers down. Nathan seemed fun-loving on the outside, but he was hiding something deadly. Her money was on him being the most dangerous. Cole opened the front door and let everyone in. He led them to the kitchen, and everyone sat around the table.

"Can I get you guys something to drink?"

"They won't be here long enough" Cole answered angrily.

Ignoring him, Zoey got up and went to the fridge. She pulled out four beers and walked back to the table, where she set one down in front of each of them. Zoey pulled out the chair next to Cole and sat. They sat in silence until Zoey said, "I take it you're here for me?"

"Zoey!" Cole bit out. He gripped his beer, staring at his brothers. "Why are you here? I haven't seen either of you in eighteen years."

"Nineteen, to be exact, and Zoey's partially right —we're here because of her, not to take her but to help you guys."

"Yeah?"

"A lot has changed over the years, but you wouldn't know that, would you?" Bryson asked.

Zoey reached over and gripped Cole's hand. "Did your uncle tell you what I did?"

Bryson took a sip of beer. "No. We have people watching Cole at all times."

"What the fuck!" Cole yelled.

Nathan rolled his eyes at Cole's response. "Like I said, a lot has changed."

"That doesn't explain how you are watching me or who is watching me. I sure as hell know I don't have a tail."

"Detail on you is not easy. The government trained you well, but I also have my ways." Bryson smirked.

"Let's put our dicks away and get back on track," Zoey snapped.

Nathan picked at the label on his bottle. "Why don't we get your friend Tex on the line, and he can help explain. I have a feeling you will trust him more than your own brothers."

"Tex?" Cole asked. "I'm not sure I know a Tex."

"Fine." Bryson pulled out his phone and pressed a button. The phone rang a few times.

"I told you I would call once I talked to your brother." Tex's Southern drawl came over the line.

"Tex, what the hell is going on?" Cole asked.

Zoey could hear the sound of Tex typing on the keyboard; each stroke echoed through the phone. "Since you finally let me start to dig into your background, I connected some dots. Let's say my contacts at the CIA had a lot of information about your brother."

"What do you two have to do with the CIA? If you are here for help, I'm out of the military."

"Ohh, brother, we aren't here for help. We're here to help you." Nathan's smile disappeared and was replaced with a deadly expression. "See? You weren't the only one to serve your country, but I never left my family or brother to deal with the hell alone."

"It wasn't like—"

"Doesn't matter what it was. We need the thumb drive Zoey has."

She reached in her pocket and clutched the thumb drive harder. "Why do you think I have the thumb drive?"

"I have a man working on Clyde's team, and they have a video of you downloading something. Do you?"

"Maybe."

Tex's voice came through the phone. "Zoey, these men might be assholes, but I've looked into them, and they aren't going to go against us. Do you trust me?"

She trusted Cole the most, and if Cole was on board, she would give them the information, but she wanted a copy first. "Cole, do you have an extra thumb drive and computer?"

"Yes," Cole stood and handed her his gun. "If they try anything, shoot."

Zoey looked at the gun he handed her. God, she hoped she didn't have to fire the weapon. It hadn't worked out for her so well the last time. Cole had helped her putty the bullet hole in the wall—she had missed him by three feet. Now, she was glad the bullet had gone very wide, but she wasn't confident in her ability to take anyone out.

* * *

Cole

He practically ran to his office to grab the USB. He felt like his world was being turned upside down. When Cole left his childhood home, Nathan was a goofy teenager. Bryson had always been serious. The verbal abuse was directed mostly at Bryson, and Cole received some, but not as much. Their father seemed to leave Nathan alone.

From the deep lines under Bryson's eyes, nothing seemed to have changed. *Why would Tex say they're trying to help?* He grabbed the drive and headed back to the kitchen. Cole planned to demand some answers before Zoey handed over what she had. He placed his computer and thumb drive in front of Zoey and sat down next to her.

"While Zoey does what she needs, I want some answers before we show you what she has."

Zoey fired up the computer.

"It's been so many years. You've missed a lot of what happened," Nathan said.

"Well, I'm listening and want to know," Cole said.

Bryson smiled sadly. Cole knew he wasn't going to like what his brother had to say. He recalled the incident with his dad that had made him decide to leave. Typically, a father would take his son to a sporting event for fun, but Marcus had taken him to Vegas and used him to get intel on a competitor. When he couldn't find what he needed, Marcus had beaten the guy until he signed over part of his business. That was the moment Cole knew he wanted nothing to do with his father.

"My first year at Harvard, I was approached by

the CIA to help take down Samuel Highmore. It was easy for me to get into any event around the world. When Nathan turned eighteen, they brought him on too. The two of us used our connections to help take down some evil in the world."

Samuel Highmore had run a pyramid scheme that stole millions from his clients over the years. Cole knew about the story because his friend Antonio Ross had lost money to Highmore. Antonio also came from a wealthy family, but he'd still gone into the Navy. He owned a mercenary company in Fort Lauderdale. The always-grumpy guy settled down with his wife. Cole chuckled inwardly thinking about the last time he talked to Antonio he complained she wouldn't stop feeding her kills to the gators. She was a retired assassin for the CIA. But Cole knew the story, and Mr. Ross took down Samuel Highmore.

Cole leaned back in his chair, "Why would the CIA take on a case on US soil, and furthermore I know Mr. Ross was the one to take him down."

Bryson nodded, but before he could answer, Tex's voice came through the phone. "Come on, Cole, you know the CIA works on US soil all the time. Mr. Highmore did go down because of your brothers, but they couldn't admit to the public what they'd done. Mr. Ross worked with the CIA to make it look like it was him."

"Okay, you work for the CIA," Cole announced, more for himself than anyone else in the room. "What are you doing here now? You could've come to me years ago, but why now? And what do you want on the USB?" Zoey hadn't told him what she had yet, but he assumed it was terrible, especially if the CIA wanted to get their hands on the information. Every muscle in his body was tense as he waited for the answer.

"We've watched you for years, and you've made a good life for yourself. Neither one of us wanted to bring you into the issues at home. The government hasn't let us bring our family down, because they worry it will draw too much attention to us. So instead, we work to keep Father under control and in the background, which is easier now since he is getting close to retiring."

"This is why I hate the CIA. Sometimes I think they are as corrupt as Dad."

Bryson narrowed his eyes. "Our father will pay for what he did. You can count on that." Something flashed across his older brother's face. If Cole weren't watching every move, he would've missed it.

Not saying a word, Nathan looked out the window.

Cole took a deep breath. "Sorry, I've worked years to forget about my past, and it wasn't you guys I ran from—it was him. And I have so much hatred. Then when I tried to contact you guys, I was told you wanted nothing to do with me. Calling you to help with Bella took everything in me."

Nathan fisted his hands. "There is so much you don't know—and believe us, we weren't the ones who didn't want to talk to you. However, we can talk about all that later. Zoey, can you show us what's on the drive?"

She pushed one of the thumb drives into her pocket. He liked that she'd made a copy. She turned the laptop so everyone could see and clicked on the MOV file. Cole reached over and grabbed her hand.

A gruesome movie played out before them. Clyde Walker stood to the side, ordering his men to brutally beat Senator Cramer. Zoey had stopped watching after the first hit. Screams came through the video. Clyde kept asking where the product was. Cole figured he was talking about drugs. Nothing else would make someone beat and kill a man.

Cole watched in surprise as his mother walked onscreen in a white dress and high heels. She didn't even flinch as she walked over to the man in the chair and stared down at him.

He grabbed the mouse and skipped back a couple seconds. *This can't be right.* His mother was a drunk who liked to party. *She wouldn't be able to stomach watching something like this.* If he hadn't seen it with his own eyes, he would not have believed anyone. *Was my childhood a lie?* He kept his eyes on the scene, watching as she ordered Clyde to put a bullet through the senator's head. Clyde Walker wasn't the devil—Cole's mother was.

A couple things clicked into place. His brothers had shown up because they knew he might see the video. They'd come to protect their mission, nothing more. His anger bubbled over. He wanted to kick them out. "You didn't come to help. You came to protect *her*."

Bryson closed his eyes and let out a sigh. "There is so much more than we have time to discuss. The hit on Zoey's head is gone. Nobody is looking for her anymore. One day, I hope we can sit down and talk about everything."

"Tex, is the hit gone?"

"Yes."

Cole let out a sigh.

Bryson grabbed the thumb drive from the

computer, pulled out a gun, and aimed it at Zoey. "I need the other USB."

Cole ground his teeth and went to reach for his gun, but Nathan had one pointed at him. Zoey slowly reached into her pocket and pulled out the drive. She was as pissed as he was, and if she handed it over, all their evidence would be gone.

Nathan grabbed the second drive, then he and Bryson left. When the door clicked, he grabbed his gun.

Zoey held him back. "It's not worth it."

"I'm going to kill them."

ZOEY

"Where are you guys going tonight?" Bella asked.

Three weeks had passed since Cole's brothers took Zoey's only evidence. They had removed the hit from her head, though, and she hadn't heard another peep. Zoey was able to search for a job again and maybe find an apartment. Cole had said she could live with him as long as she needed. They had become close, but she wanted to stand on her own two feet and date Cole. Some days, she felt like she was living off him even though she'd started to do the books for the flipping company.

She'd gone to her first interview at a defense company the week before, and they'd called to offer her the job this morning. To celebrate, Zoey and Cole were going out to eat. With access to her bank account, along with her new job, she would be back on her feet in no time. She still looked over her shoulder every second, waiting for the other grenade to drop. Things had gone away too quietly. Cole said he felt the same way. He didn't trust his brothers—hell he didn't even know them at all. Tex had been shocked when Cole said his brothers had pulled their guns. He was working to find anything.

Cole had taken Zoey to the range a few more times. Now, she carried her own gun—a SIG Sauer—tucked away in her purse. The time they spent at the range was filled with sexual tension. He would wrap his arms around her and help improve her aim. She had a feeling he liked her in his arms as much as she loved being there. The tension between them was high. Neither one had pushed passed kissing, but it was getting harder and harder not to rip off his clothes.

Tonight would change everything. She planned to spend the time in his room and finish tiptoeing around the attraction. Zoey glanced across the room to see him talking to Ian.

Zoey thought about Bella's question. She didn't really care where they went, as long as she ended up in Cole's bed at the end of the night. Since the first time

Cole had saved her life, she'd gone to bed dreaming about the man. Numerous times, she'd stopped herself from crossing the hall and climbing into his king-size bed. He walked around the house each night after dinner with a low-hanging pair of sweatpants and no shirt. *It should be illegal to look that good.* The weight she lost while being on the streets was starting to come back. If Cole had a say, she would eat ten times a day. She felt better as her curves began to come back.

Bella tapped Zoey's hand, pulling her eyes from Cole and Ian. "From the way you're eating him up with your eyes, I would have to guess you're not thinking about where you are going to eat tonight," Bella joked.

She felt her face turn red. Smirking, Bella leaned against the living room wall. They had become close friends over the past few weeks, and for the first time, she knew what a true friend was—even if she gave her shit a lot.

"Look at him… I don't know if I can wait for tonight."

Bella scrunched her nose. "He is good-looking, nothing compared to my Ian. I can't believe you made it this long without jumping him. You should get a medal or something."

"We're going to stop and see Paul before heading to Bohanan's Prime Steak and Seafood."

Zoey grabbed a nail and pounded it into the wall. She and Bella were putting the finishing touches on the house before it went up for sale. She'd entered the house at the lowest point in her life, and now they were finishing it to be sold when she was on the verge of being the happiest she'd ever been.

"I love that place. Ian took me there not too long ago." Bella's eyes immediately went to Ian, and her eyes lit up every time she talked about them. She'd told her the story about her old boss over drinks one night and how Ian and Cole had come to the rescue.

"Do you think this place will sell?" Zoey asked, changing the subject.

"I already have a couple families ready to look. They've been hounding me for a house in this neighborhood for a while, it should go quick."

"I'm going to be sad to see this house sell. I know this is your business, but don't you ever get attached to the house?"

"Some of the houses, yes. Things happen, and it makes it hard. A few of the houses, I can't wait to get rid of." Bella shrugged. She grabbed the abstract teal-and-silver painting and placed it on the nail.

"Cole said you guys already found another house."

Bella stood back and adjusted the painting so it was straight. "Yes, the auction isn't until the end of next week. I think we might pick up a couple more houses. They are talking about hiring another team so we can do more."

Cole had mentioned his thoughts about how he sees the company in five years. He has a plan to turn the two-man flipping team into a large company. They really wanted to start with an apartment building soon.

"I've spent the last three weeks helping, and it was fun, but every muscle in my body hurts. I can't wait to start my desk job again, where the only muscle I work is my brain." She would miss working with Cole every day, but when they came home at night, they would be able to talk about their days. Cole had told her a few times that she didn't have to work and could do the company's books. She planned to continue helping them, and one day, if the company became as large as Cole wanted, she would work for them. Until then, though, she wanted to work full time.

"Do you have plans tomorrow?" Bella asked.

Zoey had planned to spend the weekend getting

ready for the new job on Monday. "No, I just have a few things to get ready for work on Monday. Do you want to meet and have lunch?"

"Yeah, my friend Caroline is back in town for a couple days, and her husband Wolf is coming in, as well. You didn't get to meet her last time, and I figured the boys are going to want to hang with Wolf. We can have a girls' night out."

The last time Zoey enjoyed a girl's night out, she'd let her ex-friend Sarah talk her into taking a job with Clyde Walker. She imagined things would be different with Bella—they wouldn't go to a club and wear dresses that were way too short for their age. Nope. They would go somewhere they could talk and get to know each other.

"That sounds like fun. I've heard Cole say nothing but good things about Wolf and Caroline. I can't wait to meet her."

"Has he told you the story about how they met?"

"Nope. Cole hasn't told me the story about how Caroline and Wolf met, but he told me the story about how Wolf saved his life in North Korea and if it weren't for him, he wouldn't be alive today." Zoey knew she would be dead if not for Cole. So in some weird twist of fate, Will had saved her life too . She threw a couple teal pillows onto the rented couch.

The furniture helped people picture what it would be like to live there.

"He saved Ian's life, as well. I'll let Caroline tell you her story. It's almost too crazy to believe."

"Like stealing a video of your boss killing the senator to later find out your boyfriend's mom gave the instructions?"

Bella burst out laughing. "Yes, exactly that crazy."

Ian and Cole waved them over. It would be her last time in the house. Cole must've been thinking about the same things, as he wrapped his arms around her and rested his chin on her head. They both stared at the house silently for a few minutes before turning and heading to the car. A new chapter would start for them.

* * *

All night, Cole had treated her like a princess, pulling out her chair and making sure everything was to her liking. The restaurant was to die for, and the bottle of wine he ordered was so good, she drank too much before realizing it. She stood and wobbled on her feet. Cole was holding her a second later, with one hand on her shoulder and the other wrapped around her.

Later, Zoey lay on the couch next to Cole in his media room. Cole ran his hand along her arm as they watched the latest Avengers movie. She had no clue what was going on in the film; her thoughts were on his fingers and how they was sending pulses through her body. Cole was so easy to talk to, and when the conversation came to a lull, the silence didn't make her uncomfortable.

Tex had called to let her know everything was still okay. They both checked the news each day, and his brothers hadn't used the video to take anyone down. Cole was still upset they had pulled a gun on her. He didn't care about himself. He only cared they had a gun on her.

Paul had called while they were at dinner, and on the way back to the house, they'd called him. He was so excited to say his son and grandson were coming to visit. After another scare with his health, he'd decided it was time to reach out to his family and get to know them again. She hoped Cole's brothers were trying to protect him. She wished he would talk to them again one day, but after the gun incident, it would take a lot of talking to let those men near her again.

The movie ended, and Cole clicked off the TV.

His hand running down Zoey's arm sent a chill down her body. "Ready to call it a night?"

"Hmm… No…"

"Are you sure?"

"Do I need to buy a flashing green arrow?" Zoey teased.

Cole spanked her ass lightly. "Smartass, I don't want to rush you or do anything you don't want to do."

Zoey had already fallen for Cole, and his words made her fall a little farther. She was done waiting. She wanted him almost as much as she wanted her next breath. "I would tell you if I wasn't ready."

"Really?" He ran his finger over her tight nipple. She had changed into a white cami and shorts, opting for no bra, and her nipple poked through the thin material.

"Yes." The word came out breathlessly. He was barely touching her, and her body wanted more.

"Like this?" He ran his thumb across her nipple again, and she could hardly take the little bit of touch he was giving her.

"More." She wanted his hands all over her body.

He quickly flipped her to her back, and he was propped up above her, using his forearm to hold up his weight. He lowered his head, brushing his lips across hers. "Did I tell you how hot you looked tonight?"

Not saying a word, Zoey nodded.

He pressed his hip against her, and his hard member pushed against her. "I've been hard as hell since you walked out of the bedroom wearing that black dress and now here with this white cami. I can barely control myself."

"I want you, Cole."

Those must've been the words he wanted to hear. He pressed his lips to hers, demanding entrance. She was so lost in the kiss, she almost didn't even realize he had her in his arms and was heading down the hall. He kicked the door to his bedroom then gently placed her in the middle of his bed.

ZOEY

Last night was more than Zoey could ever have wished for. Cole had taken care of her like she was the most important person in his life. Tonight, she was meeting Wolf, the man who'd saved Cole and Caroline. Zoey was nervous about meeting Caroline —she sounded so strong and empowering.

Bella had reassured her a million times that Caroline would like her. She still couldn't shake the nerves, and they planned to meet downtown, near where Zoey used to live on the streets. Tonight, she would walk by the alley where Al had died. He'd lost his life because of her. Paul and Cole tried to tell her it wasn't her fault, but it still bothered her.

Zoey took a couple deep breaths and looked in

the mirror. Her lips were swollen from kissing Cole the night before. She'd never experienced that kind of passion, and she couldn't wait to spend another night with him. He'd been so in tune with her body. No man would ever make her feel the same again, and she didn't want to be with anyone other than him. Zoey knew she was falling fast and deep for Cole and last night she had almost blurted out that she loved him. Luckily, she'd kept her mouth shut. She didn't want to scare him away by telling him too early.

This morning, he had brought her breakfast in bed. He'd made her french toast and bacon with a side of fruit. She'd once told him as a joke that she wanted breakfast in bed for her work on the house. Her jaw had dropped as he walked in with a serving tray and her food. Each bite had been delicious. The man wasn't only sexy as hell, he could cook.

Tonight, they were going to a local Irish pub called The Muddy Pub and Grill. It was a place Ian and Cole liked to hang out. It was laid-back and had good beer and even better food.

Zoey held Cole's hand as they walked toward the entrance of The Muddy Pub. She didn't realize how hard she was squeezing his hand until he stopped and pulled her in his arms. "Wolf and Caroline will love you."

Before she had time to respond, he pulled back and opened the large wooden door to the pub. He placed his hand on her lower back and nudged her through the door. "I hope you're right," she mumbled as she stepped through the open door.

"Stop worrying. You and Bella have become great friends. I don't understand why you think Caroline or Wolf won't like you."

Everyone had talked so highly of the couple, she was worried she would make a mistake or that they wouldn't like her. She didn't want to do anything to affect Wolf and Cole's friendship. "You're right. I'm probably being stupid. I just want them to like me."

Her heart beat a mile a minute as they walked through the pub. Cole's hand on her lower back helped calm her nerves. She wasn't the best at making friends, but now that she had Bella, she didn't want to do anything to mess it up. Cole's friends liking her meant a lot. She took a deep breath as he walked her to the large table at the back of the pub.

A couple sat with Bella and Ian. They laughed at something the other man at the table said. The woman sitting next to the man rolled her eyes before laughing along and placing her hand on his. He turned and smiled at her, and the expression held so much love.

A waitress walked up to the table and pulled out her pad. She was a few inches taller than Zoey's five-eight. Her blond hair was pulled back into a long braid down her back. She rested her hip against the table and laughed at something Ian said. Bella held out her hand and the waitress shook it.

"That's Amanda. She served two tours in the navy. Last year, her unit drove over an IUD, and it took out her convoy. She's trying to work herself back into society. It's not always easy and she struggles a little more from the accident."

Zoey's heart went out to her, and she immediately wanted to pull the woman into her growing circle of friends. When the woman turned and smiled at Cole, it wasn't flirtatious. It was a smile to a friend, and Zoey couldn't help but smile back. As she walked closer, Zoey noticed a big red scar down the side of Amanda's face. It didn't take away from her beauty, but Amanda reached up and ran her hand over it self-consciously.

"Hey! I was just grabbing their drinks. What can I get you?"

Cole leaned forward and gave Amanda a one-armed hug as he still held onto Zoey's hand. "You look good, Amanda."

She huffed. "You mean the scar doesn't look so Freddy Krueger-ish today."

Cole narrowed his eyes. "You know that's not what I meant."

"I know. Sorry. It's hard not to think about it. What can I get you two?"

It looked like Cole wanted to say more, but Zoey could tell she wanted to drop the subject. "Hey, Amanda. I'm Zoey. I will have a jalapeño margarita if you can make it."

She smiled warmly at Zoey and let out a relieved breath.

"I will have whatever's on tap," Cole ground out unhappily. He went to say more, but when he started to open his mouth again, Zoey squeezed his hand.

The waitress quickly left. Zoey knew there was more to Amanda's story. The woman needed help, but Zoey could only imagine she wasn't going to ask for it. She wanted to follow her and ask her what she could do, but Cole placed his hand on the small of her back and pushed her toward the table.

She smiled when they reached the edge of the table. Everyone stopped talking and looked at them.

Her worry set back in. Starting the conversation always felt awkward, but when she got talking with someone, she could talk for hours.

"Hey, guys," Cole said to his friends. "You know Ian and Bella. This is Caroline and Wolf. She's worried about meeting you, so be nice."

Zoey could feel her face turn red. She hadn't expected him to say that to Wolf and Caroline.

"Hey, Zoey, it's nice to meet you," Wolf said.

"It's so nice to put a face with the name. I've heard such great things about both of you."

Cole pulled out the chair across from Caroline. The woman smiled at her before saying hello. Her warm smile eased some of the butterflies in Zoey's stomach. Cole settled into the seat next to her and rested his arm across the back of her chair.

"Everything will be fine," he whispered in her ear.

Zoey couldn't hold back the smile. Cole worried more about her than anyone else. She knew he wanted everyone to get along, but he told her he wanted her to have fun and not worry about what anyone thought. Sometimes that was easier said than done; little voices in her head sometimes made her second guess the things she said.

The waitress returned and placed the drinks around the table. Zoey took a sip of her margarita and enjoyed the heat from the jalapeño.

"How did you guys meet?" Caroline asked.

"I purchased a house off the auction block." Cole took a sip of beer before he continued. "I went to take a look at the house, and when I went into the master bedroom, she shot at me."

"Wow, you guys started out with a bang," Wolf said. "Sorry, couldn't help the bad joke." He laughed.

Cole let out a laugh and finished telling the story to Caroline and Wolf about his uncle and his mother. He even told Wolf about his brothers showing up. When he mentioned their names, the vein in the inside of his neck pulsed. He was still pissed at his brothers. Zoey wasn't sure how she felt. They had gotten the bounty off her head, and no one had shot at her or come after her.

"Are you still having Tex monitor everything?" Wolf asked.

Cole nodded. "Yeah, everything went away too easily. I kinda feel like the other shoe might drop, like everything is too good." He wrapped his arm around her and pulled her in tighter.

Ian placed his beer on the table. "I still can't believe your brothers pointed a gun at Zoey."

Zoey was surprised by how angry Ian's words came out, he was also mad she had a gun pointed at her. It had happened so many times in the past four months, she was more worried about something happening to Cole than to her.

"Yeah, I don't know what I will do if I ever see either of those two men again," Cole said. "You never point a gun at a woman. He could have explained they needed both drives. What they did was uncalled for."

She knew one thing: no matter what they said, she wouldn't have given up the thumb drive. They'd taken it the only way she would've given it up.

"You know if you need anything, the team would be here in a second," Wolf told him. "And if we are away, you know Ghost and his team is not far away. They would help. Don't take this on your own. If something doesn't feel right, follow your gut."

Zoey was in awe of Cole's friends. She didn't know what to say. This wasn't Cole's issue as much as hers. She was the one to take the video and a copy of the dirty accounting books.

"If we need help, I will call, but you guys are still in the military. I'm not going to jeopardize your jobs," Cole said. He held up his hand when Wolf was about to say something. "I'm using Tex, and if I can't handle what comes at us, I will call, but it will be bad if I call you in."

Zoey stiffened. Jesus, he'd thought the threat wasn't over either. She could tell Cole had been on edge, but not how much until then. She didn't want to add to his stress, so she'd kept her feeling about the uneasiness in her stomach to herself.

Cole turned toward her, his pupils dilated. He looked tense and ready to attack. She worried that if someone did come after her again, Cole and his friends would get hurt because of her. Zoey didn't know what to do, but she wanted to spend as much time with Cole as possible.

Just talking about the what-ifs, Zoey scanned the interior of the bar, although she wasn't sure what for. Her training as an accountant hadn't given her the ability to read a room. Over the last half hour, she had noticed Wolf and Ian looking around the room. They had picked a table in the back corner, giving them a good view of the whole restaurant. She hadn't realized that until right then. She thought back to the previous night, when Cole had asked the waitress to change their table to one in a back corner. "You guys pick tables to watch a room. Do you always do this?"

Caroline smiled at her, making her feel at ease

for the question. "Yes, Wolf hates when we can't get the seat in the back so he can watch the place."

Wolf squeezed his wife's hand. "I don't like when I can't fully protect you."

"Because someone's going to grab me at the ice cream shop," Caroline joked.

Wolf's brows drew together. "You were taken at a bar, your friend had a bomb strapped to her at the grocery store, and someone tried to put a sleeping agent in the ice on a plane."

Caroline frowned for a second. "You're right. I shouldn't have joked about that."

On the way over, Cole had told the story about Caroline smelling the ice in the cups from the flight attendant and it smelling wrong. He was able to signal his teammates not to drink anything on the plane. The airplane would have been hijacked, and Caroline had helped save many lives that day. Zoey was in awe of the woman, and meeting her in person was even better.

"Cole told me earlier about the plane. I can't believe how brave you are."

Caroline shifted in her seat. "Instincts kicked in when it was the heat of the moment."

The night continued, and Zoey relaxed. Caroline

and Wolf were terrific people, and she understood why Cole liked them so much. Bella thanked him again for helping save her from the crazy people who'd kidnapped her and taken her to San Francisco. She was enjoying herself, and when she saw Amanda walk into the bathroom, she wanted to talk to her. Not sure if it was the second margarita, she had a little courage.

When she excused herself, Caroline joined her. "You know us women can't go by ourselves." She turned to her husband. "We'll be back."

Bella waved and stayed with the three men.

Caroline gripped Zoey's arm and leaned in. "Are you going to talk to the waitress? You saw the way she was acting, didn't you?"

Zoey wasn't sure she understood the meaning behind Caroline's question. "You're not going to stop me. I think she needs help, and even if it's an ear, I'm going to try. I've been the one thinking nobody was here for me, and I don't want to see someone else go through that."

A smile spread across Caroline's face. "I like you. No, I noticed it earlier too, and I've been waiting for her to take a break. Now let's go find out before Wolf figures out what I'm up to."

The two women headed toward the bathroom and waited outside the stall for Amanda to finish. When she walked out, she had tears running down her face. She quickly wiped them away when she saw Zoey and Caroline. "Oh, I didn't hear anyone come in."

"Why are you crying? Who did this to you?" Caroline demanded.

Amanda stepped back and flinched.

Zoey stepped forward and took her hand. "We were both worried about you. Something seemed off, and we wanted to know if you need help."

She let out a sigh. "The only help I need is a plastic surgeon. No… sometimes, the customers can be rude, but in time, it will get easier."

"Fuck them," Caroline said. "You're beautiful, and if they can't see it, who cares? They only say mean things to make themselves feel better."

"That would be easier to think if I didn't have this down my face." She pointed to the scar.

After taking a quick glance around the empty bathroom, Zoey said, "You are gorgeous, and when you find the right man, he won't even notice the scar. Is that all that's bothering you?"

The woman glanced back at the door. She crossed her arms across her body and let out a sigh. “Nothing is the problem. I’m just having a bad day.”

Zoey didn’t believe her, but she wasn’t going to call her out. Instead, she reached into her purse and pulled out a piece of paper and pen. “Here is my number. Call if you need anything or even someone to hang out with.”

Caroline grabbed the piece and quickly wrote down two numbers. “That number is mine, and the other is a man named Tex. If you need help, he can help, no questions asked. Tell him I gave you the number.”

“Thank you,” Amanda said before rushing out of the bathroom.

“She’s hiding something.”

Zoey nodded. “But she doesn’t know us well enough to let us help.”

The next thing she knew, Caroline was hugging her. “You’re one of the good ones. Cole’s lucky to have found you.”

Excited to have made another friend, Zoey laughed. “I’m happy I shot at him.”

Caroline laughed and grabbed her hand, then they walked back toward the table.

When they arrived back, Wolf looked up at his wife. “Did she need help?”

Caroline smiled and sat next to her husband. "She wouldn't tell us what's wrong, but we gave her our numbers and Tex's number. I'm not sure she will call."

"Wait. How did you know?"

Wolf looked at his wife. "She's been eyeing the waitress since we arrived, and I saw her go into the bathroom, and all of a sudden, you wanted to go. When she was at the table earlier, I could tell she was hiding something, and I saw Caroline pick up on it."

Zoey shook her head. "I wish she would've told us something."

"She will." Cole paused. "When she is ready."

"I hope she does…"

Ian set his beer down. "It was great catching up, I think it's time to head out."

Zoey looked down at the silver watch Cole had bought her. Three hours had passed. "Wow, time flew."

Everyone got up from around the table, and Caroline handed Zoey a piece of paper with her number on it. "Call me whenever. If you make it out to California, the other women would love to meet you. Maybe you and Bella could come out and stay with us." Cole grunted, and she added, "You're always welcome over, Cole."

The men threw a stack of bills on the table—more than enough to cover the tab. She knew it was to help Amanda out. Cole and his friends had hearts of gold.

Zoey's cheeks hurt from smiling as they walked out of the bar.

ZOEY

Cole stood at the edge of the bed, looking down at her. She squirmed under his heated look. Instead of covering herself up, she slowly pulled the cami up a little.

"You're so fucking gorgeous," Cole growled.

She never felt like the prettiest woman, just average. Before meeting Cole, she'd always felt lost in the crowd of single women. But he made her feel like the prettiest woman each day. Not one day had passed without him telling her how good she looked. Hell, he didn't even have to say the words—he told her each day with his eyes.

"Come here."

He crawled on the bed next to her and pulled her to his hard chest. She slowly ran her finger down his tattoos. She loved the colorful art. His arm was covered with cartoon characters—Daffy Duck, Pluto, and Popeye—but it was the tattoo inside his arm she traced. "What made you choose to get this one?"

"I got that when I returned from North Korea..." Cole's voice broke for a second. He ran his hand over the tattoo. "I wanted something to remind me how lucky I was to make it out. Four other men weren't so lucky. If you look right here"—he pointed to four dog tags—"each one represents a brother I lost that day."

Zoey traced over the four tags with her finger. "Someday, I want you to tell me about each one of them."

He pulled her hand away from his tattoo, brought it to his mouth, and kissed it before he tugged her on top of him. She immediately felt his erection pushing between her thighs.

"I'm so happy to have my hands all over your body. It has killed me the last month with you sleeping in the room across the hall." He wrapped his hands around her and brought her close, so his mouth was next to her ear. "The other night, I got up to get a glass of water, and I heard you moan my name. I almost lost it and barged in. Instead, I came back here laid in bed and wrapped my hand around my cock."

She'd never been with someone who was so verbal, and they were still dressed. The tips of her ears turned red in embarrassment. She couldn't believe he'd heard her, but she was so turned on knowing he'd come back and jacked off because of her.

"What were you thinking about while you laid here in bed?" she whispered in his ear. Cole brought out a side of her that she hadn't known she had. He pressed his hips up, rubbing himself against her.

He slowly worked his hand up her side, dragging her cami up her body. Goosebumps trailed his fingers as they lightly grazed her body. She helped him pull the cami off and toss it to the side. He sat up and buried his face between her boobs. The quick motion caused his hard member to press against her clit, and she flexed her back, pressing her boobs against his face. His five-clock shadow brushed against her skin, sending another sensation mixed with his hot breath and tender touch.

"Gorgeous," he murmured as he ran his hands down her bare back. Her reply was stuck in the back of her throat when his warm lips wrapped around her nipple.

Cole raised his hand and gripped her other boob, slightly pinching her nipple. She couldn't hold back the cry of ecstasy, from the pain and pleasure mixed together. Each second, the world around them disappeared; it was only them. Nobody was after her. Nobody needed anything. It was only them.

The feeling of his hands on her body finally was too much. She rubbed herself against his erection. Cole dropped one hand from her boob and grabbed her ass, slowing her movement down.

She whined in frustration. "Cole, I need mor—" She breathed as he ground upward, hitting her clit.

She could feel the smile against her skin as he moved to her other nipple and took it in his warm mouth, putting it between his teeth and nipping before ravenously sucking. A light sheen of sweat broke out on her skin. Her yoga pants and his shorts were too much between them. She wanted his naked body pressed against hers. She slowly pulled back from Cole and sighed in frustration when his mouth left her. Zoey grabbed both sides of Cole's shorts and worked them down his body. She stopped and licked his cock for a second as she peeled off his shorts. She'd brushed up against him over the few weeks and had felt his hard cock, but she hadn't realized how big he really was.

"Cole." She giggled as he pulled her back up his naked body. Her hard nipples rubbed against his body, sending pleasure through her. Zoey was so close to the edge, and they had barely touched each other. She couldn't wait until he was inside her.

"These need to come off." His voice was low and growly.

Not wanting to lose the connection, she quickly jumped to the side to pull her yoga pants down. She was in such a hurry to get back to him, her foot was stuck, and she toppled over. Zoey ignored the chuckle from the bed and finished pulling off her pants. Standing next to the bed, Zoey could feel how red her face was.

Smiling up at her, Cole pulled her back onto the bed. "Come here."

She straddled him, loving how their skin touched. The sensation made her feel even closer to him. He gripped her hips, keeping her from rocking back and forth. She wanted a release so bad and didn't know how much more of the teasing she could take.

"Slow," he said softly. "I want everything to be perfect."

"How about we go slow next time?" she countered.

Cole chuckled, reached up, and pinched her nipple. She loved how he could play her body. The slight squeeze followed by a caress was sending her wild. He dragged his finger down from her nipple to between her legs, not removing his other hand from her hip, keeping her in place. She felt on display for him, and not in an awkward way. She had no desire to cover herself up. She wanted Cole to watch her lose it from his touch. As he slowly worked his thumb against her clit, she could feel the wetness around her folds. Cole took his time playing her like a fine violin—circle, circle, then pressure and repeat. He was no longer holding her leg in place, and she spread herself wider across him as he reached up to caress her boob.

She couldn't take it any longer—she needed Cole inside her. Zoey rested one hand on his chest and rose onto her knees. Cole's finger never left her nub as she reached for his hard member, placed it between her folds, and slowly worked her way down. They both groaned in unison. Cole's thumb continued to give her so much pleasure. He sat up and took her nipple in his mouth as he fully entered her. Nothing had ever felt so good. Her body was on fire. Masturbating to the fantasy of him was nothing compared to having sex with him.

"Damn," Cole gritted out as he lay back down. "You're better than anything I could ever have dreamt up. God, I could lay here all night, watching you ride me."

Each word turned her on more. She picked up her speed along with Cole's thumb rubbing tightly against her. She was close to the edge. She was trying so hard to fall over but wasn't quite there. "More…" she breathed out.

Cole pushed harder and faster on her clit. The extra push was all she needed. She closed her eyes and arched her back, and the pleasure rolled over her. Cole never let up. His thumb still did circles as she rode out her orgasm.

"God, you're sexy," she heard him say. Zoey was so far lost in her own pleasure that the words sounded far away.

When the fog started to settle, she pulled his hand away and pressed her lips to his. Her hard nipples pressed against his body. Panting, she continued to rotate her hips.

"I've never seen anyone sexier than you. Damn, you are a wildcat." He placed a hand on each of her cheeks and set the pace. It was slow and steady. It felt like they were becoming one as she kept rotating her hips.

"You feel so good," Cole growled.

She flexed her inner muscles, and Cole closed his eyes, pressing his neck back. She loved how he was losing it. She repeated the motion again.

"Faster," he pleaded.

Zoey sat up, resting both hands on his chest, and worked herself faster on his shaft.

"Fuck me, Zoey," he encouraged.

Zoey didn't need to be asked twice. She hadn't been with a lot of people and felt inexperienced when it came to sex, but Cole brought out a different side of her.

"Feels… so… good. Just like that."

Her body felt like it was out of control. She could feel the fire building again. Cole reached down and circled her nub while pinching her nipple. The dual sensation took her out of her mind.

"I'm close," she whispered.

Then he flipped her over onto her back. His motion was so quick, he never left her. Cole pushed deep into her, and she wrapped her legs high around his waist, matching each thrust with the same energy. She reached between them, pressing her clit. He stopped to watch for a second. His pupils dilated, lost in the pleasure.

The sound of his thighs slapping against her was

loud, and the sound of him breathing made her even crazier. She'd never been so turned on before. Cole lowered his head to her nipple and took it into his mouth.

"Yes... oh, that feels so good." She screamed before tipping over the edge a second time.

Cole continued to thrust into her. Zoey's body felt like jelly as they came together. She clenched her muscles, and Cole thrust a couple more times before pushing far in her and stopping. They were both sweaty and breathing heavily.

Sex is messy and such in a good way. There was nothing she would change about her first time with Cole. It was equal parts dirty and passionate.

When Cole caught his breath, he captured her lips and kissed her long and hard before slowly pulling out. She whimpered.

Cole swore, "I'm sorry, Zoey."

She looked at him puzzled.

"We didn't use protection."

She turned to the side. "I have an IUD, and I haven't slept with anyone in a long time. I'm clean. Not saying we should always skip protection, but we are fine as long as you are clean."

He leaned in and gave her a long, slow kiss. He

pulled her tighter against his body. "I'm clean, and it's been a long time for me, as well."

Something stirred in her stomach about the fact that he hadn't been with anyone. She was falling for him hard and fast.

"Sleep," he whispered.

Zoey turned so her back was to him, and he pulled her in closer. Their skin touching, they fell asleep. Zoey went to bed, feeling like the luckiest woman on the planet. Cole woke her three times throughout the night to make love.

COLE

Cole and Ian stood on the steps of the Bexar County Courthouse. Six days had passed since they had drinks with Wolf and Ian. Zoey had started her new job on Monday, and she was so excited every day to tell him about work. He didn't' understand everything, but he enjoyed listening to her. Cole missed her during the day while he was at work. He liked listening to her hum a different tune while she worked. Everything had been going well until he received a call from Tex on his way to the courthouse.

"You mean those assholes think you will meet with them as long as they go through Tex?"

"Yes," Cole responded angrily.

"You want me to come with? There is no reason

to go to the meeting alone. Tell me when you're meeting, and I will come."

"I need to handle this. If, for some reason, Tex thinks it's a setup, I will call you, but until then, let me deal with this," Cole told Ian.

"I don't understand how they got the whole hunt for the Senator shut down, and the video never came out. No one had even mentioned the funeral or a memorial for the man. How deep in the CIA are your brothers, because a lot of strings needed to be pulled to stop the media?"

"Never crossed a CIA agent I trusted," Cole said. "But I need to take the meeting to make sure Zoey is still safe. I owe my brothers a moment of my time, as I was the one who left them. Don't get me wrong—I plan to come fully loaded to the meet."

A smile stretched across Ian's face. "You're going to pay them back for their little stunt. Oh, after the meeting, they will never pull a gun on her again. Now are we going to buy a house or keep talking about my situation?"

An auctioneer walked out onto the steps of the courthouse, and everyone gathered around. Bella wasn't with them. She was at the house inspection for the home they'd just finished. Bella had showed it to a few people before listing it, and the place was under contract before it was even officially on the market. They weren't expecting any surprise with the home inspection, and the closing was likely to be finished in the next couple of weeks.

"Two hundred," Ian shouted out above the crowd.

Cole smiled when a few people groaned and glared in their direction. They usually won the houses they wanted. A few people would way overbid because they wanted the home for themselves and weren't looking to make a profit.

"Sold to Bidder Twenty-Six," the auctioneer yelled.

There were two other homes on the block today; Cole and Ian wanted to see what they went for. If the price was right, they might pick up the other two. They had hired a few more men and planned to start doing multiple projects at once. They had Bella trying to find them an apartment building to turn into a rental instead of a flip.

"Eighty thousand," the auctioneer announced.

When no one bid, Ian raised his hand. "Well, that was way less than I thought it would go for."

"The place needs a total rebuild," Cole grumbled. He wasn't entirely excited about the second house, but they could still make a profit.

"You going to tell Zoey about the meeting?" Ian asked. "She's going to want to come with you."

"I figured she would. I plan to tell her afterward."

"Not sure if that is the best idea. You've been taking her to the range a lot. She might shoot you this time if she finds out you talked to them and didn't let her know, especially since the meeting is probably about her."

Cole ran his hand through his hair and started to walk toward his SUV. "I don't want her to worry."

Ian followed, shaking his head. "I always have your back, man, but I think you should tell Zoey because when she finds out, she's going to be pissed you didn't tell her."

Cole snorted. "'Pissed' will be an understatement, but I would rather have her pissed and safe."

Ian shrugged. "No matter what I say, you're not going to change your mind. So when you have to grovel, make sure you know her favorite color, food, and flower."

Cole couldn't help but smile. "Purple, steak, and daisies."

"Well, at least you know what you're going to need to make her happy."

"Thank you."

"I'm always here for you."

Cole leaned in and hugged his friend. "The meeting's on Monday. I will be late coming to the job."

"Call if you need me."

On the ride home, Cole put the meeting with his brothers out of his mind. He was excited to go home and get dinner ready for Zoey. He wanted to celebrate her first week of work. The flower store was on his way home so he stopped and picked up a bouquet of daisies.

* * *

Zoey

When Zoey pulled up to the house, Cole was waiting by the door. She'd known the auction was in the afternoon, and she hadn't been sure she would make it back before him. She parked his BMW in the driveway. Earlier in the week, she'd had to talk him out of taking her to the dealership to buy a car. He thought the BMW was too old. It was way better than the vehicle she had pawned to stay in a hotel for a week before the streets, though.

Cole was holding white daisies.

"Oh my god, I love them."

"They didn't have purple, so I got white." Cole congratulated her on her first week of work.

Zoey rushed with her flowers into the kitchen and put them in water. She didn't even care what kind they were. No one had ever brought her flowers, so Zoey was excited to get any, but he'd remembered from the first day when she mentioned daisies.

"They're perfect." Zoey smiled as she put her nose into the bouquet. She knew she would have to move out soon, not because she didn't want to keep dating him. But she didn't want him to feel obligated to let her live with him.

Cole held up two bottles of wine. "Red or white?"

"White." She ran her fingers over her lips and walked across the kitchen. "I really appreciate everything you've done for me."

"You don't have to thank me. Sit. I have dinner in the oven. While I get it ready, tell me about your day."

"I really enjoy working there. I know it's only the first week, and every job is fun for the first week, but I think I'm going to like it. The CFO and I sat down today and went over the upcoming year's budget. She was impressed with my knowledge and wants me to think about becoming a CPA. She said the company would pay for it."

Cole took a sip of his wine. "That is amazing. Is that something you want to do?"

"Yes, but it is a lot of work, and what happens if I don't pass?"

"I have faith in you. Hell, I will help you study."

"I'm going to think about it." She tapped her fingers on the wine glass. "Tell me about the house—did you get it?"

"Yep and another one," Cole grumbled.

"Oh, the one we drove by the other day?" The house had looked straight out of a horror movie. She'd joked with Cole that it would be better to bull-doze it.

Cole leaned against the kitchen counter. "Yep, nobody bid on the thing."

"Can you take me by the other one this weekend? I want to see what it looks like before you guys perform your magic. It's crazy how much a few things can change those houses, and pictures don't do justice to what you guys do."

Cole leaned over and brushed a hair out of her face. "You helped with the last one."

Zoey closed her eyes and leaned in to his touch. "What did you say?"

Cole smirked, "I said you helped."

"My arms still hurt from all that painting. Who needs a gym membership when you could take up painting?"

Cole rounded the counter, placed his hands on Zoey's shoulder, and squeezed lightly. It felt so good. "Don't stop."

He leaned down and placed a kiss behind her ear, sending a shiver down her spine. Zoey let out a moan.

Cole ran his tongue along her ear. "I miss watching your ass sway at work while you used the roller. I only got half my work done when you were around."

"I miss working with you, but not the physical labor," Zoey replied.

"Enough about work. Let's eat and have a fun weekend."

Cole put his glass of wine down on the counter and walked back to the stove. He took a lasagna out of the oven, and the smell filled the kitchen.

"The smell alone is making my mouth water."

"It should be good. I didn't make it. I picked it up from the Italian restaurant on the corner."

"Louie's Lasagna?"

"Yes."

Zoey jumped off the stool, walked over next to Cole, and wrapped her arms around him. He turned in her direction, and she pressed her lips to his. The kiss was soft.

He pulled back and rested his forehead against hers. "I love the attention, but what did I do?"

"Everything."

Cole's pupils dilated. She was hungry but not for food. She wanted her man, and him having dinner ready with flowers was a huge turn-on. She had never dated a man who did as much as Cole had for her. Most of them could barely open the door or pay for a meal.

"If you don't step back, we will never eat."

"I'm fine with eating later."

"Zoey," Cole ground out.

She smiled up at him, and she knew he'd decided to not worry about dinner.

"Well, I guess you will be my appetizer."

She let out a loud squeal when he wrapped his arms around her and lifted her onto the counter. His hands pushed her dress up her thighs.

"Bedroom," she breathed out between kisses.

Cole smiled against her lips. "I want my appetizer in the kitchen."

Zoey blushed. She'd never been with someone in

the kitchen. It sounded so dirty and turned her on even more. He deepened the kiss, and his touch on her legs was sending her over the edge. She wouldn't last very long, and she was completely dressed.

She tried to scoot closer to the edge to rub against Cole, but he held her in place, not letting her move.

"Please," Zoey murmured against Cole's lips.

He pulled back. "I will take care of you." Cole worked her panties down her legs. Her ass was on the cold counter.

Cole wasn't lying when he said she was going to be his appetizer; he took her over the edge over and over. Dinner was cold by the time they got to it, and neither of them cared. It was the best end to her workweek and the start of their weekend.

COLE

Cole gripped his drink as he watched his brothers. He'd told them to meet at his house. He wanted to have an upper hand this time, with no audience. Cole sat with his gun on the table. His older brother rolled his eyes when he sat down.

"I'm not even armed," Bryson grunted.

"You're lucky I'm even speaking to you after you pointed a gun at Zoey."

Bryson winced. "We needed everything, or there might have been a chance you'd continue the mission without us. This is something we've been working on for years. Does Zoey know we are here? I would really like to apologize."

"No, I'm never letting you around her," Cole grumbled.

"Dude, I can tell by the way you look at her you're going to marry her, which will make her our sister. You can't keep us away forever. Now that we know some of the things we were told were lies. You've been told lies, as well."

"So what lies was I told?" Cole asked bitterly.

"We never got the calls. Mom told us you stole millions from the family and then joined the military. A year after you left, there was a raid on the house, and she told us it was you. We didn't understand Mom was dirtier than Dad. Yes, he was a piece of shit, but the things we have on Mom make him look good. He wasn't doing what he did by choice—she has always been behind everything."

"He could have walked away," Cole said.

Bryson ran his hand down his face. "No, she has everything. She would have killed him on the spot, and who knows what would happen if he wasn't there to buffer us?"

None of this makes sense. He'd watched his dad kill and torture someone. "Believe me, I've seen what our dad is capable of. I've witnessed it firsthand."

"I told you he wouldn't believe us." Nathan threw his hands up in the air.

"You talking about the trip to Vegas? Think back

to the day. Someone else was in the room," Bryson told him.

Cole wracked his brain, but all he could see was the man in front of him bleeding to death, while he couldn't do anything to help him. His dad had put the man through hell, and he remembered hearing a faint laugh in the background, though he couldn't place it.

"I don't know what you're talking about." He could remember the smell of the blood, but not if there was someone else in the room.

"Mom was there."

"No, she…" He faintly remembered someone else but didn't know who it was. *Why would she want her kid to see that?* "Why?"

"She's fuckin' crazy!" Nathan exclaimed. "Each one of us went through it, and to top it off, she had it all recorded. A few years ago, we came across the tapes. You left a week after the incident, and she fed us full of lies. For once, she gave us attention we'd never seen before, and it was all a ploy to make us hate you. Hell, it worked for years. Then when we put all the pieces together, we didn't want to drag you into the mess."

"Now?"

"Well, your girlfriend kinda dragged you into it

now. We are going to take mom down. I promise you that, and the evidence you gave us helped, but we…"

Cole had worked enough missions to know his brothers wanted Zoey's help. "No."

Nathan looked over at Bryson and shrugged. "You don't even know what we were going to ask."

Cole snorted. "I was a Navy SEAL. You want to use Zoey for something. You didn't come here to see me or try to work shit out. The CIA only cares about their mission and nobody else."

Neither of his brothers seemed to care he was upset. They acted like he hadn't even raised his voice. "We do want to get to know you. Hell, it's been years, but you're right—we've turned into the mission. We want to take the bitch down so bad that we will risk everything. That isn't fair to you and Zoey, but we can't do this without her help."

Cole clenched his hands together. "Tell me what you need so we can figure out another way."

"We need her to get into the computer at Clyde's place, and before you say anyone can hack it, that's not true. He's paranoid and doesn't have it connected to the internet. The info Zoey retrieved the first time helped, but we need more. We are sure he didn't wipe out her retina authorization. She was the only one besides Clyde who had access. He's out of town. We can sneak her in, log in, and make a copy of the remaining files. There is more evidence on the computer, and if we wait too long, it might be gone. I overheard him talking about a fail-safe on the hard drive—it will erase if removed."

"She is not going to do it."

"Will it take everyone down this time?"

Cole's head whipped toward the kitchen door.

Bryson nodded.

"I will do it."

"We can find another way."

"No, you can't. That computer is locked down, and your brothers are right—he hasn't removed me, because I set up the protection on the machine. He was moving everything from his safe files onto the computer. He destroyed the other copies. There's no other way."

Bryson stood from the chair and gave Zoey a hug. "Thanks, Z—"

Cole grabbed Bryson's shirt, pulling him back. Bryson stumbled, but Cole pulled his arm back before forcing it forward. His fist connected with his brother's jaw. Bryson grabbed his jaw and let out a few cuss words.

"Cole," Zoey yelled before rushing to his brother.

He wrapped his arms around her and pulled her back.

He knew he was acting like a teenager, but his family had put a gun to Zoey. Now they were asking her to put her life in danger for a mission. *A fucking mission!* Cole knew first-hand how they could go FUBAR—short for "fucked up beyond recognition"—and he didn't want to put Zoey in danger again.

She wiggled in his arms, pressing her ass against his dick. He couldn't control himself around her. She twisted in his arms. "Really?"

"You were the one wiggling."

She huffed and tugged harder. Once out of his grasp, Zoey stomped over to the freezer, pulled out a bag of peas, and tossed them to his brother. "What about my hand?"

She narrowed her eyes. "Did you know they were coming here today?"

Cole reached out and tried to pull her in, but she walked to the other side of the counter in the kitchen.

Bryson chuckled. "You have your hands full."

"Oh, don't think you're not on my shit list. Your Christmas present is going to be rocks this year. I haven't forgotten you held a gun to me. But you"—

she turned toward Cole—"forgot to mention we were having guests today, and if I hadn't forgotten my phone here, I wouldn't have come home for lunch and known what was going on."

"I was trying to protect you… These fuckers didn't tell me what they wanted, and if they did, I wouldn't have even allowed them in my house."

Zoey sighed and slid into one of the chairs around the table. Cole took the one next to her, and his brothers sat across from them, the same seats they'd sat in the last time his brothers were there. Today, if his brothers pulled a gun, they wouldn't make it out of his house alive.

"I'm not a little kid you need to protect. Your brothers are trying to take down your uncle, and he needs to go to jail. The info on the computer will also help take down others. I can't sit back knowing I could do something to help." She reached over and squeezed his leg. "You know, if it were you needing to go in, you would do it in a heartbeat."

She was right—if his brothers needed another person, he would do everything to help. Putting Zoey in danger was not at the top of his list, though.

"Can we come up with a different way?"

Both of his brothers said, "No."

Bryson continued. "We've tried everything to get

the information and lost our only informant on the inside. Clyde is back in town tomorrow, and we think he knows we're on to him. He will erase the info when he gets back."

"Tonight?" Cole growled. "We haven't had time to prepare or come up with a plan—hell, I need to buy her a vest."

"We took care of everything, including the vest," Nathan said, tapping his finger on the table.

Cole still didn't trust his brothers. "Ian and I are going with; no way will I let Zoey go alone with you two. I haven't forgot about you holding a gun to her."

Bryson nodded. "Will you help us, Zoey?"

She narrowed her eyes and looked over at Cole's brothers. "Yes, but I want to talk to Cole in private."

"Sure, we will go grab the things from the car."

Nathan stood, "We really did try a different way. Zoey is our only option, and I promise I will take a bullet for her." He didn't wait for a response before turning and walking out of the kitchen, following Bryson.

"You don't have to do this, Zoey. Please, let's find a different way. I don't want you to put yourself in danger. You mean way too much to me."

Zoey squeezed his hand. "I want to do this. We've been watching every day for your uncle to be taken down. If we can get what they need, I have to help, but I wanted to run something by you first."

"Okay," Cole responded immediately.

"Caroline mentioned Tex has a way to track her and the other women out in California. I don't think we help unless Tex can have a tracker on all of us. Ian coming along is a good idea. I'm still not sure if I trust your brothers one hundred percent. They haven't given us a reason, besides being cleared by Tex, and he is pissed about the gun incident."

Cole pressed his lips to hers, catching her by surprise. The kiss wasn't soft. It was demanding and full of passion. He wanted to take her upstairs for being so kind and caring, putting herself in the line of danger to help others and take down his uncle.

"God, I love you." He paused for a second. "I know it's soon, and I had a whole thing planned, but we're not going into a dangerous mission without me telling you first. You don't—"

Zoey put her fingers over his lips. "I love you too."

"Really?"

"Yes, but—" He pressed his lips to hers again.

She rested her head against his chest. "But we are a team, and hiding your brothers from me is not being part of a team. We need to make decisions together, even if it is to put me in danger."

"Okay, next time you're going to be put in danger, I will let you know." Cole winked at her. "Now let me go call Tex real quick."

"Hopefully, we can figure out a tracker thing quickly," Zoey said.

The conversation with Tex was short. He had the address pulled up and was looking into it while we got ready. He found a technology store that had a few trackers. Ian was picking them up on his way over to the house. When Cole asked him for help, Ian didn't even ask questions before saying he wanted to help.

After his call, he walked back into the living room to find Zoey dressed in tight black yoga pants and a tight black long-sleeve shirt. Her long hair was up in a ponytail. She was sexy as hell. He groaned as his pants became uncomfortable. It would be a long night.

COLE

Zoey held the bulletproof vest in front of herself. She'd never imagined having to wear one. This was the first time she'd held one in her hands. It was heavy, and the fabric wasn't soft. She slid the vest over her head and tightened the Velcro straps around her waist.

Cole walked in, wearing a matching vest. He pulled his T-shirt over his head, covering it. The tattoos on his arm peeked from below the sleeves. He looked sexy as hell as he holstered his 9mm.

He grabbed her hand and walked her to the other side of the truck, which was parked down the street from their target. The planning for the mission was incredible. The men sat around the table with laptops, looking at every entrance. Tex was on speakerphone, feeding them more information. She sat back and took in every word. Bryson and Nathan were convinced nobody would be at the warehouse; everyone was supposed to be in Las Vegas. Cole wasn't taking any chances and made everyone go through exits and worst-case scenarios a few times. The sky was pitch dark, and the moon was behind the clouds, making it hard to see. Only a flickering light pole gave off light.

"If you don't want to do this, let me know, and we will get back in the car and leave," Cole told Zoey. The hairs on the back of his neck were standing up. Something didn't feel right, but he went through the plan and knew it like the back of his hand. He and Ian had talked. Nathan and Ian were watching from the outside, and Bryson was coming with them to get the information.

"I want to do this."

"Fine, but if one thing doesn't go to plan, we're leaving, and my brothers can go fuck themselves. The information isn't worth more than your life. There is always another way, though it might not get the information as fast. CIA doesn't like waiting, and that's the reason we're doing this now. My brothers have been in way too long. They see everything as an OP, and life doesn't always work that way."

Zoey smiled at him. "I know Cole. You've told me a million times you will stop the operation if you don't like where it's going."

"Yup, now tell me, does the vest feel good, and where is your gun?"

"The vest is heavy, but I think it's good… never worn one before." She laughed. "Never imagined I would need to wear one." She turned to the side to show her gun holstered. They had been to the range a few more times, and her shot had improved. Cole was more confident she would hit her target this time. He hoped it wouldn't come down to that.

"Stay by my side. No matter what goes down, you save yourself."

Zoey nodded, but Cole still worried she wouldn't run if something happened to him. He pressed his forehead against hers. "I love you," he whispered before pressing his lips to hers and pulling her in close. The two thick vests kept them apart. Cole reached up, ran his hands through her hair, and deepened the kiss. He didn't want it to end. For a second, he let the world around him fade away and focused only on the woman in his arms.

A whistle echoed down the sidewalk. Cole pulled away and kissed her one more time on the lips before turning and flipping his brother off. He didn't need to look to see who'd whistled. Bryson had done the same shit growing up. Some things never changed, and it brought a smile to his face. He was going to run a mission with his brothers. It would have been better if Zoey weren't part of it.

Cole grabbed Zoey's hand, and they walked over to where the three men were standing in full tactical gear. Ian handed Zoey a helmet with night vision goggles. The tracking devices Tex had found for them were pill types. Ian, Zoey, and Cole all swallowed a pill, and Tex let him know they were online. His brothers didn't need to know about the trackers. He still didn't trust them completely

"Everyone ready?" Bryson asked.

"Let's do this." Ian sounded a little too excited.

"Yes," Zoey replied as she buckled the helmet into place.

Ian and Nathan broke off to get into place. They were to feed the team information from the outside. The building was supposed to be clear, with no one inside.

After a couple minutes, Ian's voice came over the comm, letting them know it was clear. He placed his hand on Zoey's lower back as they walked down the side street to the back door. Bryson pulled out a lock-picking set and went to work on the door. Cole wouldn't say it out loud, but he was impressed with how fast he'd gotten the door open.

Bryson took the lead, Zoey was next in line, and Cole brought up the back. They lowered the night vision goggles when they stepped into the warehouse. Cargo canisters were stacked three high, and rows of pallets wrapped with plastic. Cole squinted at the writing on one of the boxes. Columbia coffee. He knew better than to think it was only coffee in the containers.

His brother held up his fist, giving the signal to freeze. Cole's heart pounded. On any other mission, he would have been ready, but Zoey was along. He dropped his fist after a beat and motioned for the others to continue. The office was in the back of the warehouse. They needed to cut the video feed.

Tex's voice came over the comm. "The panel is to your right, on the wall." He was wired into a video feed on Bryson's helmet. The team needed him to walk them through cutting the camera without setting off an alarm.

Six more steps, and they were at the panel.

"Take off the cover." Bryson pulled out a small screwdriver and removed the cover. Cole couldn't tell the difference between the wires running in the panel.

"Cut the yellow and the green at the same time."

Bryson rolled his neck before placing both wires in the cutter, and he squeezed. "Done," Bryson told Tex matter-of-factly.

"Camera is done. You have five minutes before any triggers will go."

They moved toward the back of the warehouse. When they were a couple feet from the door, they heard a loud crash, everyone froze. Bryson quickly opened the door to the office and cleared the room.

"Go," Bryson demanded. "I will go see what's going on."

"Four minutes, thirty seconds," Tex said over the comm.

Cole wanted to assist his brother, but he wasn't going to leave Zoey alone. He nodded, and his brother took off back the way they came.

Zoey quickly walked into the room and sat behind Clyde's desk. When she moved the mouse, the computer turned on. She raised the night vision goggles and put a device up to her eye. A red light scanned her eye, and the screen changed to the desktop. Any other time Cole would've been impressed with the technology. Not so much today. He handed her two thumb drives. She looked at him puzzled he held up two fingers hoping she understood he wanted a copy for himself.

When she smiled at him, he knew she understood. He kicked himself for not explaining earlier. It was a last-minute idea when he grabbed one of the devices from his drawer. Just in case his brothers didn't do anything, he would give the other drive to Tex. He was done waiting for them to do what they needed. He wanted this part of his life ended.

They watched as the bar moved across the screen one minute left on the computer copy. He watched the office door and waited for his brother to return. Zoey reached up and pulled the thumb drive out of the computer as Bryson walked into the room. She quickly shoved one into her pocket and held the other out to Bryson. He wasn't alone. He's big brother had a tabby cat in his hands.

"You taking the cat with?" Zoey joked as she scratched behind the cat's ear and it let out a meow.

"Incoming. Two black Mercedes just pulled up outside," Ian said over the comm.

Bryson quickly dropped the cat and pointed toward the door. "Let's head out the back exit."

Cole lowered his night vision goggles and followed Zoey. "If we come under fire, Zoey, you run."

He let out a sigh when she nodded. They crouched next to a container when the door they'd entered earlier flew open. In walked his uncle and the three men Cole had fought in the alley. They were headed back their way.

Bryson motioned for Zoey and Cole to follow. They slowly walked around the container to the edge of the warehouse. Cole could see the exit only twenty feet away when he heard his uncle complain about the lights. He didn't have time to tell Zoey to flip her goggles up when the lights came on, making it hard to see.

She stumbled on a box in front of her, falling to the ground, and let out a small yelp. It wasn't deafening, but one of the men heard it. He could hear them coming. He helped Zoey stand and flipped her goggles up so she could see.

Bryson motioned for us to head toward the door while he covered our backs. He held Zoey's hand with one hand, his gun in the other, and pulled her toward the exit. With each step, Cole heard his uncle's men getting closer. He dropped Zoey's hand to open the door.

When his fingers touched the door handle, the alarm in the building sounded. Loud horn sirens squealed through the building. Clyde yelled for them to turn off the alarm. They used the distraction to get the hell out. Once outside, the three of them ran down the street toward the cars.

"We are out," Bryson said over the comm.

"On our way," Ian growled back. His partner wasn't happy about the unexpected guest, either.

Nobody said a word as they rushed down the street. Cole tugged at Zoey's hand to get her to run faster. He wanted to get the hell out of there. He also wanted to get back to his house and see what was on the thumb drive. Cole planned to give the info to Tex, so he could make sure it was taken care of properly.

Cole opened the door to the SUV, pushed Zoey through the door, and shut it behind him. When he rounded the corner, he stopped and looked at Bryson. "You better take him down tomorrow. I'm not going to wait much longer before I take things into my own hands."

"I got you, brother." Bryson leaned around and gave his brother a hug—the first one in years. "I promise to take them down."

Nathan gave Cole a two-finger salute before jumping into the SUV. Ian climbed in next. Cole turned the key and took off without waiting for his brothers. Cole squeezed the steering wheel, partial pissed the mission wasn't as easy as it was supposed to be. They hadn't been caught, but it'd been too close, and his adrenaline was high.

Cole hit the phone button on his steering wheel and barked out Tex's name. The phone rang once before Tex's voice came over the line. "Jesus, that was close. I'm trying to figure out what went wrong, because your uncle is also in Las Vegas. I'm not kidding. There is a man identical to your uncle sitting at the craps table in Vegas. He's on my screen. We need to figure out who this man is and when your uncle set this up. Nobody had been to the warehouse all day, and someone shows up when you did. Did you give the info to your brothers?"

Zoey smiled at Cole and handed him the drive. "Yes, but we made a copy for ourselves. It was a last-minute decision, and I wasn't sure we were going to be able to pull it off. But when Bryson left the room, to go check out the sound the cat made, we were able to make a copy for ourselves."

"Damn." Cole could hear the smile in Tex's voice.

"Once we get to the house, we will upload a copy to you. I want to know what is on the USB, and if Bryson doesn't hold up his end of the deal, I know you will do what it takes to get something done. That was close, too close, and I'm not putting Zoey through that again." He reached over and grabbed her hand.

"I will send you a secure link where you can send the data."

"Thanks."

They talked for a few more minutes before hanging up. The car was silent for the rest of the drive. Cole was watching every car behind him. Something still felt off, and he wasn't sure what would happen next.

ZOEY

"Does this mean it's over?" Zoey asked as she curled up on Cole's lap. "Your uncle looks pissed, but not as mad as your mom. I have to give it to her—she looks good for someone going to jail. Most of the time, the press photos are bad, but she looks like she's almost Photoshopped."

Cole and Zoey were sitting in his media room, watching the latest episode of *Impractical Jokers*, when Tex sent Cole a text, telling him to turn on the news.

"She does look a little smug for having her hands cuffed behind her back. I'm a little mad my father isn't in cuffs. Tex is going through the files to see if my brothers missed something."

Eighteen hours ago, she'd helped steal the data

they needed then gotten up and gone to work. They both decided to stay in and wait for the news to break on the evening news report. Cole wanted his brothers to push for the arrest, but he'd told Zoey he didn't think they would get it done quickly. "Maybe your dad isn't as bad as you remember."

Cole closed his eyes and rested his head on the back of the couch. "That's the thing—I left when I was eighteen, and for the next eighteen years, all I saw was my mom throw charity events and drink. My dad, on the other hand, left at night, and numerous times I saw him with blood on his clothes."

"Your brothers said she set him up to do it."

Cole shook his head. "That might be the case, but they aren't telling us everything, and I'm hoping this wasn't some ploy. Bryson has so much anger underneath."

She had noticed how Bryson watched Cole's every move. They'd said they were going to take down his mom and they had. "We have to give them the benefit of the doubt."

"I still don't like it," Cole ground out dryly.

"I know," she conceded. "But the bad guy is in jail, and I don't have to worry anymore."

"And Senator Cramer's family was informed about his death." Cole sighed.

"Maybe I should look for an apartment this weekend."

Cole didn't say anything for a few seconds as he ran his hand down her arm. She loved living with him, and they had worked so well together. They were dating and loved each other, but how long would that last? She worried he only felt obligated to let her stay because his family had tried to kill her.

"Do you not like it here?" Cole asked, and she could hear the hurt in his voice.

She'd never meant to make him feel like she didn't want to be there. "I love living here, but you asked me to stay because I was homeless and your family was after me." She bit her lip before continuing. "I have money again, and your family is behind bars."

His blue eyes met hers. "I don't want you to leave. All along, I wanted you at my house. Something about the first time I saw you, it clicked. I'm not going to force you to live with me, but I want you here in our house and in our bed."

"I want to stay," she said.

"Good. Now that we have that solved, we can

finish watching the police send my uncle and mother to jail."

"Did you and Ian work on the house today?"

"Yeah, it should be a quick flip, but I might need to work over the weekend. If you want to spend Saturday with Bella, you can. I'm sure Ian won't have a problem if it's just us working."

"How about I come help instead, and if we finish earlier, we can go to the pub for dinner and have Ian and Bella come along?"

She enjoyed spending time with his friends. Caroline had sent her a text that morning, asking how she was doing. They'd texted back and forth for a little while before she headed into work.

"Are you sure?"

"Yes, I actually miss working at the house with you." She took a sip of wine. "But don't get me wrong—I love my day job."

"It's demo work, so these arms will get a workout." He squeezed her bicep.

Last night, when they were leaving the warehouse, she'd seen a group of people sleeping on the sidewalk, and she couldn't stop thinking about it at work. "I want to help at a home shelter or something."

Cole didn't say anything right away. He ran his

hand up and down her arm. "I have a friend who runs a foundation, and I could talk to them about opening a shelter in San Antonio, but we would need to run it."

"I don't know the first thing about running a shelter or where to get the funds from. It would be amazing, but I wouldn't know where to start."

Even the mention of the idea made her head run with possibilities, but each one scared her to death. She wished she could have found a place to help her when she was on the street but had no clue where to turn. Cole casually mentioned the Ross family name like he wasn't sure she would know who the family was. She did know the Ross family was rich, and not the new-money rich. The family had more money than they knew what to do with. They had opened a women's shelter in Fort Lauderdale. It'd made headlines because Antonio's wife was also the heiress to a large fortune.

"I'm sure Kat would come out and help. Not sure I would leave you alone with her." Cole chuckled. "She is a retired assassin and is known for taking out men who hurt the women who come to her shelter. Last time I talked to Antonio, he was grumbling that she'd fed another body to the gators in the back yard."

"You're joking, right?" Zoey asked.

"I'm sure her husband wishes I was joking, but she promised to stop killing since she is six months pregnant," Cole added.

"I'm not sure I can do it, but I would love to talk to her about the possibilities or even finding a place to help at."

"Anything you do will help. It was an idea. I planned to bring it up the other day after I talked to Antonio. He was the one who sent the guy to watch over Paul."

"That's right. I wished I could have thanked him before he left." Everything had been so busy, she hadn't made it over to introduce herself and thank him for helping. That morning, after Cole told Antonio everything was clear, he'd caught the first flight back home. Antonio had said they had a mission in South America and could use John's help.

Zoey and Cole watched the news a little longer, and when everything was just being repeated, they turned it off and went to the bedroom.

* * *

Cole

Later that night, Cole's phone dinged on the bedroom stand. Bryson had sent a text, asking him to meet outside. Cole grabbed his gun from the nightstand and headed for the door. "It's the middle of the night."

Bryson pushed his way in, went to the kitchen, and grabbed a beer out of the fridge. "I know."

"Why not make yourself at home?"

"I need a beer, and you're going to need one, as well."

Cole didn't like where this might go. He grabbed one and joined his brother on the couch. "What happened?"

"We did everything to the fuckin' T. There is no way she should've gotten off—and this quick."

Cole had a sinking feeling who he was talking about. "I watched the news before going to bed, and she was cuffed and taken in. No one is released that fast."

Bryson nodded solemnly. "I called a few contacts, and she didn't even get processed. Someone escorted her right out the back door. That's not even the fucked up part." Bryson took a long swig. "I need something stronger."

"What is worse than her getting out?"

"Nathan's gone."

"You think he helped her?" Cole was glad he'd kept an additional copy of the drive. Tex was still spending time going through everything, and maybe he could find something. He rolled his neck to release some of the tension, but it only worsened.

"Yes, I think he helped her, and I'm worried he said something about you. When they were arresting her, she made a comment to Dad that he needed to take out your girlfriend before she told anyone the info she had. Zoey has something else that we don't know about. What is she keeping from us?"

"She helped you break into a building and steal data. Why the fuck do you think she has something else?"

Bryson pinched the bridge of his nose. "I don't know. Hell, I don't even know who to trust anymore."

"That's the thing—how do I know I can trust you?"

"You have no reason to trust me." Bryson tilted his head to the side. "I thought I could trust Nathan, and I think I can. He's doing something to protect us. Not sure what. But he always feels like he owes me, and I'm worried about what he got himself into."

"Why does he owe you?"

Bryson shook his head. "Not my story to tell."

"And you want me to trust you." Cole narrowed his eyes and took another sip of beer. "It's tough when you keep leaving shit out and only telling half the story."

"Fuck!" Bryson took the last swig of his beer. "Everything will come out in time. I'm going to find them. I came to warn you to watch Zoey and tell her to watch her back."

Bryson stood. "Don't say anything over your phone. Hell, I would sweep your house for bugs, just to make sure."

And he was gone as quickly as he'd come. Zoey was in danger again, and they had no clue what he was going to do. He knew he couldn't order her to stay home and not go to work.

Zoey padded out into the kitchen and sat down on his lap. He spotted her out of the corner of his eye when his brother sat down. Cole was sure Bryson had heard her, but he didn't call her out. He loved having his hand wrapped around her. She gently laid her head on his shoulder. "Well, that sucks."

He burst out laughing. So many other words ran through his head, but "sucks" was accurate. "Yeah, I suppose I can't talk you into quitting your job, moving into a safe room, and letting me lock the door."

"Nope, but I'm racking my brain about what your mom thinks I have. You know your brother actually looked hurt."

He scooped her up and headed to the bedroom as she squealed in his arms. "We can't do anything now. I'll make calls in the morning."

ZOEY

Unable to believe her eyes, Zoey stared at the NASBA webpage. Ten days ago, she'd taken one of the exams for the CPA after two months of studying nonstop. Cole would stay up and quiz her each night. She wanted to take one exam at a time, and she was looking at her score—ninety-six percent.

She and Cole had fallen into a nice routine over the past couple of months. They hadn't seen anything from Nathan or his mother. Work was amazing, and she couldn't wait to tell her boss, Ivy. The previous week, Ivy had told her she had no doubt Zoey would pass and that when she did, they would go out and celebrate.

Zoey quickly took a snapshot of the screen and sent it to Cole. She didn't expect him to answer; he was interviewing new employees. But she wanted him to be the first person she told. She couldn't believe that four months had passed since Cole walked into her life, and each day, she fell farther for the man. She loved spending Friday nights lying on the couch in the media room, just cuddling.

Zoey couldn't be happier about how their relationship was progressing. They had talked about kids, not something she'd ever really considered. Her life wasn't the easiest growing up. Her mother had done a good job, but Zoey didn't know how good of a mother she would be. Cole had the same feelings for another reason. His parents were the worst, but he and Zoey had decided that when the time was right, they would try. They weren't in a rush, but someday, they wanted kids.

Almost every week, she and Bella got together, even if it was just to have a cup of coffee. She loved hanging out with Bella. They spent hours talking about Zoey's plan for working with the Ross family to open a shelter in San Antonio. The only problem was her job—she couldn't work full-time and run the shelter. Testing the waters with her boss, she'd mentioned her idea, and her boss had been encouraging, promising she could go part-time.

Next month, Kat and Antonio were flying to San

Antonio to talk about options. Zoey had talked to Kat a few times on the phone and fallen in love with the woman. She was a spitfire. Over the weekend, Zoey and Cole were going to look for locations. Cole's idea of the shelter was starting to come to fruition, and she was excited and nervous. Zoey was in shock how much her life had changed over the last few months.

It was almost lunchtime and Zoey was typing on her keyboard when Zoey heard the slight tap on her door. Without looking up, she told the person to come in. She heard the door click closed, followed by the sound of the lock engaging. Her spine stiffened, and she looked from the monitor to the woman standing in her office. Zoey immediately reached for her purse when the lady pointed the gun at her.

"Don't even think about it, Zoey."

Zoey clenched her fist around the arm of her chair as the woman dressed in a black pencil skirt and white blouse sat down. Her blond hair was perfectly done up. Even if she hadn't seen photos of the woman, Zoey would've known who she was the first time meeting her. Those eyes were the same as Cole's. The only difference was Cindy Walker's were hollow.

Zoey's building had tight security, so she had no clue how the woman had gotten into her office unescorted. No one was allowed to roam the halls. "Why are you here?"

"Nathan already told me you don't know about my plan."

Nathan's alive? They hadn't heard from him since the night Bryson showed up to the house. Bryson continued to run the family business and work for the CIA. The board had voted Bryson's father out of the company, and he had cut ties with his mom and dad. He'd come to visit a few times, and each time he'd looked more tired than he had the last time. When he wasn't running a mission or a billion-dollar oil business, he was looking for Nathan. Tex had put out feelers, and it was like he had dropped off the face of the earth.

"I will repeat again—why are you here?" Zoey asked while she slowly slid her chair to the side. She needed her gun; it was her only way out of the situation.

"When my oldest son turned me over to the feds, they took my money. Luckily, I've had leverage over my youngest for years. But now, I need money. Nathan can't get it without Bryson finding him. So I've come to get money from my middle child."

Cole had done well flipping houses, but far less than the Walker family was used to. "How much?"

"A billion dollars."

This lady must be on crack. No way Cole has a billion dollars lying around. If he did, he would've told her. "Not sure where you think he will find that much money."

Cindy smirked. "Next week, my son turns thirty-five, and he gains access to his trust fund. All he's going to need to do is sign it over to me. Then I'm gone. He never has to see me again."

Zoey was trying to wrap her head around the fact that Cole had a huge trust fund coming, but she still didn't understand why Cindy needed her. "What do you want me to do?"

"You're my leverage." She stood and kept the gun trained on Zoey. "Now move."

She reached for her purse.

"Stop, you don't need your things. Let's go."

Zoey cursed inwardly. It wasn't only the gun she wanted. After the night at the warehouse, she'd thrown a tracker in her purse, just in case something happened.

Cole's mother came around Zoey and pushed the gun into her back. "Move."

It was lunchtime, and the office was empty as

they walked toward the exit. No one saw her leave, and she wondered how long it would be before someone noticed she was missing. A black town car was parked outside, and Cindy shoved her into the car then climbed in behind her. Suddenly, Zoey felt the prick in her neck.

"Don't fight it."

She barely heard the words before things felt slower. Her hands felt like weights, and she was losing the battle to stay conscious. Her last thought was of Cole.

* * *

Cole

Cole leaned back in his office chair. *Another interview down.* He and Ian had been on the hunt for another project manager for two weeks now, nobody had fit what they were looking for. He reached up and tugged on his tie. He hated wearing the thing, and he disliked coming into the office even more.

Ian looked up from the file in his hand and threw it on his desk, along with the files for the other five people they'd interviewed. He glanced at his clock—it was almost one in the afternoon, and he still had four more interviews to sit through. But they wanted someone who would fit with them.

He pulled his cell from his desk drawer, and he couldn't help but smile when he read Zoey's text about passing her exams. He'd had no doubt she would pass. He replied quickly: *I knew you could do it.* He would take her out for a nice dinner to celebrate.

Cole knew she liked working at the technology firm, but once a week, they helped at different shelters. She had met so many people who needed help, and each time, she jotted down notes of where they were. Next month, they were meeting with Kat and Antonio.

Cole hated that is mother and father were out of jail and going to every function under the moon. Bryson was still working on finding Nathan. He liked talking to his older brother, even if he was a grouch most of the time.

"I'm so sick of doing interviews," Ian said.

"We will find someone." Cole didn't know if he believed the words.

"This next one was sent over from Tex. Jason, just got out of the military last week," Ian said, not looking up from the resume.

"I know, and I hope he works out. He was highly decorated but didn't put why he was discharged."

"Tex wouldn't have recommended him if he didn't trust him."

Bella knocked on the door and brought Jason in. He was the first candidate who'd actually worn a suit to the interview. It didn't matter what the job was—Cole expected everyone to dress professionally or at least put on a clean shirt for the interview.

An hour later, Cole was excited. This kid was hungry and ready to get to work. Cole looked over to Ian, and he smiled. They were both on the same page. He was about to offer him the job when Bryson charged into the office. Bella was right behind him, a worried look on her face. Bryson was dressed in a black suit, his tie loose around his neck and his hair a mess from running his hands through it.

"What the fuck, Bryson? I'm in the middle of an interview, and why the hell are you not in Dallas?"

"When did you talk to Zoey last?"

"This morning. I've been in interviews all day. She sent me a text before lunch." Cole glanced over at the clock. It was well past three o'clock. He hadn't realized they'd been talking to Jason for so long. He grabbed his phone from his drawer and saw he had a dozen missed calls from Bryson and nothing from Zoey. That wasn't normal. He quickly dialed her number, and it rang four times before going to voicemail. With a swipe, he hung up then dialed her work phone. Again, it rang then went to voicemail. "What's going on, Bryson?"

"I got a text from a burner phone, saying you and Zoey were in trouble. When you didn't answer, I jumped on the first flight here. I didn't have Ian or Bella's number."

This could all be a misunderstanding. He pulled up the website for the company Zoey worked for and dialed the main number. He asked to speak to Zoey's boss, Ivy. She said a woman had taken Zoey out to lunch; she'd figured they were celebrating Zoey passing her test and hadn't thought anything about it. When he asked what the woman looked like, Cole's heart pounded in his chest.

"She's been out for two months. Why now? " Cole asked Bryson.

The memory of Zoey that morning, her hair wrapped up in a towel, flashed through his mind. She had just gotten out of the shower. He'd felt like the luckiest man on the earth.

"I have a feeling it has to do with your birthday next week," Bryson said.

"I don't understand," Cole answered.

Bryson stared at him for a few beats. "You really don't know?"

"No."

"You come into your inheritance. She doesn't have any money. Nathan doesn't get his until he's thirty-five, and coming after me will be too public. They are cut out of the company, and I've worked over the last couple of months to shut down their streams of income. Grandfather's money went to her through the company, nowhere else. They're broke."

Broke or not, she'd fucked with Zoey, and that was unforgivable.

ZOEY

"About time you wake up." Cindy's voice was like nails down a chalkboard.

"Sorry, some mad woman injected me with some shit."

She didn't have time brace herself before the hand hit her. Cindy dragged her fingernails across Zoey's cheek, and Zoey could feel the blood trickle down her face.

"Leave her alone." The voice was weak, but she recognized Nathan's voice. Her head swung to the side. He was tied to a chair. His face was so black and blue, he was almost unrecognizable, and cuts covered his chest.

"What happened to you?" She wanted to rush to

his side. He had been gone for months, and they had suspected he was helping Cindy.

Without answering, Nathan shook his head. Zoey looked around the room. Dark-red curtains covered the floor-to-ceiling windows, blocking the view of the outside. She was tied to a chair with gold arms. *Who the hell kidnaps someone and ties them to a gold-plated chair?* The other wall had a dark bookcase full of old books. She kept hearing the faint tick of a clock, almost like a countdown. She couldn't tell where it was coming from until she looked down. Zoey was no expert, but she was ninety-nine percent sure a bomb was tied to her chest. She closed her eyes and hoped Cole would find her soon.

An older man sat on a couch next to her chair, smoking a cigar. She knew from seeing him on the news that it was Marcus Walker. He hadn't said a word since she opened her eyes. With a gun in her hand, Cindy paced the room. She looked close to being unhinged.

Zoey waited for the crazed woman to tell her what her plan was. She didn't want to aggravate her anymore. The cut on her cheek hurt. She looked at the clock on the wall—it was almost six o'clock. Whatever they had stuck her with had knocked her out for six and half hours. *By now, Cole should know*

I'm missing. She hoped he would be able to find her soon.

"Oh, him. He's trying to play the hero." Cindy huffed. "You see, I almost got taken down by your guy's little stunt, but I had someone on the inside that let me know what was going down. When I knew I would need an out, I used one of my cards. Nathan didn't know he had a daughter. All I had to do was threaten the girl's life—and bam! My youngest has me out of jail."

"Then why is he tied up?"

"He wasn't very cooperative with helping me take down his brothers. I had to teach him a lesson. I don't know how he did it, but he hid the stupid little girl so I couldn't use her as leverage. Like everything in life, though, he failed. She will be here soon, and maybe she can go boom like you two."

"I'll kill you if you hurt her."

"Such a flair for the dramatic."

Zoey let out a breath. She would rather go through hell than let Cindy put some little girl through it. She understood why Nathan had helped his mother, and she was no longer mad.

"Are we going to sit here all night, or are you going to call Cole?" Marcus asked from the couch.

Cindy stopped pacing and stood in front of Zoey.

"See, this is the good part. I'm going to meet with my son, but he won't make it to you in time."

Nathan glared at her. "You won't win."

"I always win. How do you think our family got Walker Oil when you guys were just kids? You think your father was going to take that over with how much his dad hated him? No, it was my plan that took him out and made sure your father was in a position to take over. If I would've taken his parents out quicker, they wouldn't have made that stupid will that gave you three most of the family money. That was our money, not yours."

Zoey's heart hurt for the people this woman killed and for what Cole and his brothers had to go through growing up. She didn't know how this woman could have produced three good boys.

"We have an insurance policy out on you, so when you die along with Cole's whore, we will collect even more money. Come on, dear. Time to go." Cindy grabbed her purse off the desk and looked around the home. "I will miss this place, but sometimes, we have to sacrifice things for the greater good." She turned and walked toward the door. Marcus followed, never looking Zoey in the eyes. "Nice knowing you son, and I'm going to enjoy watching my son fall apart at your funeral because the bomb will be going off soon."

She left the room, and right before stepping out the door, Marcus pulled out a phone and slid it across the floor to Nathan. He quickly shut the door. A loud crash followed by the sound of metal sliding together echoed through the room.. She couldn't worry about the crash yet. She was secured to a chair anyway. Nathan was also drifting in and out of consciousness.

"Nathan."

His eyes popped open. "I'm not sure how much time we have, and they locked us in the panic room."

"Wait, I thought you were almost dead."

He let out a huff. "It would take a lot more than her lackeys to kill me. I notified Bryson you might be taken earlier—we need to stop them from meeting her."

She looked around the room, trying to figure out how to get out of the chair. It barely moved as she threw her weight to the side. *Damn rich people and good-quality furniture.* If a poor person had kidnapped her and tied her to an Ikea chair, she could have easily broken it. *At least if I'm going to die, it will be in style.*

Zoey felt a hand on her arm and screamed.

"Damn, not so loud," Nathan complained.

"How did you get out?"

"Do you want a lesson, or do you want out of here?"

"Where is the bomb?"

Nathan gave her a sad smile before looking at her chest. "It's still around your chest."

He untied her quickly, and they ran to the door. It was locked. She looked around the room. When she pulled the curtain back, metal bars covered the window. They were in a panic room with no way out and no clue how to disarm the bomb attached to her chest.

* * *

Cole

At six thirty, they were still no closer to finding Zoey. He'd never felt time move so fast, and they hadn't seen any information on where his mom had taken Zoey. Tex was working on a mission that had gone south, but he'd promised to look for Zoey.

Bella handed everyone sodas.

Cole wanted something harder but knew he shouldn't when he was going to need all of his senses. "Why hasn't Tex called us back? I need something, anything."

Bryson placed a hand on his shoulder. "Give it time. I know it's hard."

Cole took his drink and threw it across the room. It did nothing to cool his mind and only annoyed him that he'd made a mess in the kitchen. Bella had jumped, and he felt terrible for making her scared. "Sorry," he mumbled.

Ian walked over to Bella and wrapped her in a hug, glaring at Cole. He would get an earful later, after they found Zoey. *Fuck*—if *we find Zoey.* His crazy mother wanted his money, which he didn't even know about. *One billion dollars. Who the hell needs that much money?*

Cole's phone vibrated on the kitchen counter. Everyone stopped and looked as Cole reached for the phone. An unknown number flashed across the screen.

"Tex?"

"Hello, son." His mother's voice echoed in the room, and Cole's fingers tightened around it. He worried for a second that he might break his own phone in half.

"Where is she?" Cole gritted out.

She cleared her throat. "See here, son."

"I'm not your son."

"So dramatic. I always had high hopes for you, all of you. Not one of you did anything to make me proud."

Cole suddenly worried that Nathan might be in trouble. "Where is Zoey?"

"Meet me at the Walker country club in an hour, and we can talk about your precious Zoey."

"I can't make it there in an hour. The club is at least a couple-hour drive."

He could hear her tap her fingers on the phone. "I'm assuming my first failure of a kid is in the room. If so, get a helicopter or something. He has enough of my money to get you there."

Bryson was already on his phone in the other room when she gave the location.

"Bye for now, son." She hung up.

His phone vibrated a second time, and it was Tex. "We have a location. Hold on a second." Cole put the phone on speaker and placed it in the middle of the table. "I'm putting you on speaker."

Tex's deep Southern twang rang through the phone. "I ran the number you gave me earlier. The location keeps going in and out. It's hard to get a good read, but if I had to guess—and that's what it's coming down to—it seems to be coming from your parents' house south of Dallas."

"Makes sense," Bryson interjected.

The location of the tip was different from where his mom wanted to meet. Did they plan to move Zoey or was it a trap? "Were you able to pull up any footage of the house?"

"Yes, your parents were there but left about a half-hour ago. I've tried the phone, but I think it's getting bad reception."

"Panic room." Everyone turned toward Bryson, waiting for him to continue. "They turned the study into a panic room a few years back. Ever since then, the reception sucked. Fuck, why didn't I think of that sooner?"

Cole was excited—they had a lead. "So now what? Do we go to the house or the meet location?" he asked the room.

"Both." Ian shrugged.

"I have to agree with Ian—you and Ian go to the house. No way Mom would take Zoey to the drop. There's a chance you won't give her what she needs." Bryson paused for a second. "I will go after Dear Old Mom and Dad, but this time, I'm taking care of them."

"There has to be another way. I don't want you

going alone," Cole told his brother, but he knew from the look in his eye, there was no holding him back.

"Let's call the cops this time," Ian added.

"I agree with Ian. I know some people on the force up there, and they won't make the arrest until I make the call," Tex said. "You don't know what you are walking into at that house, either."

"Fine," Bryson grumbled.

Cole could faintly hear the thud of a helicopter. Their ride had almost arrived. Cole grabbed his gun, and Bryson handed him and Ian an extra. They were heading in armed to the teeth. Bella was staying at the house and locking all the doors. Cole told her how to access the panic room if she felt like she was in danger.

The team of three jumped into the helicopter. Cole slid on a pair of headphones and was shocked for a second when he heard Tex's voice. He didn't know how the man hacked the helicopter headphones, but he hoped he could give them information on the way to the house. Because he was going for Zoey, and his mother wouldn't stand in his way.

ZOEY

"Fifty-nine minutes to figure a way out of here," Nathan murmured.

"I thought you were CIA. Just do your cutty thing and make it stop." Zoey had seen a million CIA agents do it on TV.

"Really… I wasn't trained in how to dismantle a bomb. That wasn't the reason they recruited me. They wanted someone for intel. I was trained not to give information up and how to pry information out of someone."

"How about the phone? Let's call Cole."

He pinched his brow. "Tried the phone before I untied you. No reception. Bryson, hopefully, was able to ping the phone sometime since I alerted him you were taken."

Zoey narrowed her eyes. "Would've been nice if you gave me a heads-up. Furthermore, why did your dad leave the phone, but not help?"

"He thinks he is helping, but he didn't, and when I make it out of here, I'm going to kill them both. Doesn't matter he tried. The things he's done in the past couple months are unforgivable. A bullet to the head would be too nice of a way to kill him. I'm going to make him pay." His words were filled with hatred.

"First, we have to make it out of here and figure out how to remove the bomb attached to my body," Zoey reminded Nathan. "Let me try to grab the phone and stick it through the window and see if we can get a signal."

Nathan nodded again.

She ran to the phone lying on the floor and froze. *Fuck.* Cole's phone number was programmed into hers, and she didn't remember the number. Then it dawned on her—she didn't know Cole's number, but Caroline had made her memorize Tex's. She quickly dialed the number in the phone and went back to the barred window.

Nathan raised a fire poker from the fireplace. "Stand back."

He shoved it between the bars over the window

and shattered the window. They heard footsteps in the house, running toward the door. They hadn't accounted for more people in the house. Knowing her time was close to being up, she hit Send and placed the phone on speaker before putting her arm between the bars.

"Zo… ey… Zo?" Tex's voice was breaking up, and she didn't know if he would hear anything she said.

"Bomb. Cole's parent's vacation house. Thirty minutes."

"Zo…"

She screamed the same thing over and over until someone hit her arm from the outside with so much force, it cracked between the bars. She dropped the phone, and it clattered to the ground. She fell back to the floor, holding her arm across her body, and cried. *We're not going to make it out of this alive.*

* * *

Cole

Cole sat next to Bryson in the helicopter, watching out the window. Ian sat across from him, his arms crossed. Cole was afraid they were going to be too late. He'd thought he understood what Ian was going through when Bella had been kidnapped, but he'd had no clue. His heart was beating a mile a minute. He just hoped she was alive.

The helicopter slowly descended. They were a mile from the house. Cole knew Bryson wanted their parents dead, but saving Zoey was more critical at the moment. They would figure out the rest later. When the helicopter took off, Cole's phone vibrated.

"Yes," he answered.

"Get to that house now. You have thirty minutes."

Cole took off running at a dead sprint. He heard Ian and Bryson running behind him. He should have been more worried about cover, but he needed to get to Zoey. Tex was still talking when he hung up the phone. He would call his friend back when he made it closer.

It was the quickest mile Cole had run in years, and he was surprised the two men behind him were keeping up. He was close to the house when he came to a stop. Ian hunched over next to him, catching his breath. Behind the house, he saw a man dressed in black, an assault rifle in his hands. The window above him was broken, and a phone lay on the ground.

Cole watched and waited as the guy passed back

and forth. Bryson motioned to the shrubs on the other side. His brother was going to distract the guard. Two minutes later, Bryson was in position and rustled the shrub. The guard took notice and walked toward the noise. Cole used that opportunity to wrap one arm around his neck and the other hand over his mouth. The guard struggled in Cole's arms as he slowly fell asleep. It wasn't their goal to kill anyone. Cole dropped him to the ground, and Ian went to disarm him and zip tie his legs and hands.

Cole quickly looked around for another guard and didn't see anyone. He rushed to the window, and his heart broke when he heard Zoey whimpering inside. "Zoey?"

The sound stopped immediately, and it was quiet.

"Zoey?" he said a little louder.

"Cole, is that you?" Nathan asked.

"Yes, are you guys alone?"

"There might be others in the house, but I heard another car leave not too long ago. We only have twenty minutes before the bomb goes off."

Cole's stomach dropped. Sniping someone from a thousand feet away, he could do. He could kill someone with his own bare hands. But disarm a bomb—he'd never learned that. Luckily, his long-time friend was a bomb expert.

"Ian." Cole yelled for him to come to his side and leave Bryson to finish up taking care of the guard. "I need you to walk Nathan through disarming a bomb."

"It's not that simple," he answered, running his hand through his hair. "That's not something I can teach someone in minutes."

"I don't know how to open the room."

"Come," Bryson yelled as he headed for the door to the house. "I know how to disengage the lock to the room."

Cole followed Bryson as he kicked down the door and shot the man who rounded the corner. His brother was in a hurry, and Cole wanted Zoey alive, so he didn't care. Bryson gripped the panel to the room and ripped it off the wall. He reached his hand in and pulled out a couple of wires. Next, he grabbed the knife out of his pocket and cut the wires. Nothing happened. Then when he crossed them, the lock mechanism engaged and the door opened. Cole pushed his way into the room.

Zoey sat on the floor, clutching her arm, but it was the bomb strapped to her body that stopped him in his tracks. Ian ran past and squatted down next to her. Nathan sat on the other side, his back resting against the couch. Cole didn't know how he was still awake. Bryson growled.

"Get him to a hospital. I will stay with Zoey and Ian." Cole nodded toward his brother.

Zoey looked up at him with tears in her eyes. It was enough to crush his heart. He sat down behind her and ran his hand over her shoulder. He was working on getting out of Ian's way so he could work on the bomb.

"Everyone needs to leave. We only have ten minutes left," Zoey said between sobs.

Nobody moved. "I'm not leaving," Nathan said before passing out on the ground.

"Please, Cole, I don't want you to die," Zoey said, trying to move her arm out of Ian's way.

Cole called Tex. "We got here. Ian's trying to disarm the bomb, but we are going to need a couple ambulances."

"They are half an hour out, but I was trying to tell you before you hung up. Your parents are on their way back to the house, and they have a woman and child with them."

"ETA?"

"They're pulling down the driveway now."

Cole didn't need to ask Bryson if he'd heard,

because his brother's jaw flexed. "Thank you for everything, Tex. We got this." He ended the call.

"Not trying to put pressure on you, but how much longer, Ian?"

Ian raised his head and narrowed his eyes for a second before going back to the bomb. A minute later, Ian was taking the vest off Zoey. It was disarmed, but the fight wasn't over.

Cole pulled Zoey into his arms and cradled her for a second, wiping the tears away from her face. "Here." He pushed a gun into her free hand. "Stay with Nathan and shoot anyone who walks through that door."

Zoey rested her head against his chest. "She has Nathan's kid."

Bryson growled. "Protect him for us, Zoey."

She nodded, and Cole captured her lips. He tried to pour all of his emotion into the kiss before releasing and whispering, "I love you," across her lips.

"Ian, stay with her please," Cole said.

He nodded. "End this."

"I love you, Cole," Zoey said before he left the room.

Bryson and Cole exited the house as their parents pulled up. Two men got out of the back. One was holding a small girl no older than three, and the other was holding a woman.

"You didn't think I would find out about the helicopter landing on my land?" Cindy Walker spit out. "I raised a bunch of idiots. Your precious brother couldn't even hide his whore and her kid."

The little girl was sobbing in the man's arms, and she looked just like a Walker, but not Nathan. She was the spitting image of Bryson. He glanced over at his brother to see his jaw tic.

Bryson walked slowly down the steps, and Cole followed, watching every move his mother made. She was waving her hands everywhere, still holding the gun. When she finally noticed Bryson and Cole were getting close, she turned the gun on Bryson. "Stop."

"What are you going to do? Shoot me, Mom?" Bryson asked as he took another step forward. "I don't think you have it in you to be the one to pull the trigger."

She smirked. "Try me. Take another step forward."

He did, and his mother squeezed the trigger twice, shooting Bryson in the chest. The force of the bullet pushed him backward, and he dropped to the ground. The woman in the bodyguard's arms let out a blood-curdling scream.

Cole raised his gun and shot twice—once to the head and once to the heart. He turned his gun on the guards, and they dropped their hands from the woman and child and stepped away.

The woman grabbed her child and ran to Bryson. She dropped to her knees and clawed at his shirt. Over to the side, their father watched, not moving. The little girl was crying and sobbing as hard as her mom.

"Please don't die, Bryson. Damn it, I love you."

Bryson slowly moved on the ground and wrapped his arm around the woman, "Damn, all I had to do is get shot for you to finally admit you love me?"

She sat up and glared at him, and as the little girl climbed on his chest, he let out a groan. They had all made sure to put on bulletproof vests before coming to the house.

Cindy Walker was dead, and her husband still hadn't moved from the spot next to her.

"Cole?" Zoey's voice pulled his attention away from the scene. He went to her side and wrapped her in his arms.

COLE

The aftermath of the shooting took most of the night. Police wanted a statement from everyone. Zoey had worried Cole would get arrested for killing his mother, but once Bryson told the officer about the cameras in the house. The footage proved it was self-defense, and he wasn't arrested.

Bryson had two large bruises in the middle of his chest, and the paramedic wanted him to go to the hospital for possible broken ribs. He refused to go to the hospital or to let the little girl go from his arms. Zoey fell in love with the three-year-old. Her name was Carly, and her mom's name was Cristin. Cole's mother had threatened her when she found out Cristin was pregnant, but she'd thought Cristin was sleeping with Nathan, not Bryson.

Nathan, on the other hand, was taken to the hospital. Everyone stayed until the doctor gave them an update on how Nathan was doing. The doctor planned to hold him overnight for observation.

Marcus didn't say anything to his sons; he only gave a statement to the police. He didn't cry for his dead wife or his son who'd almost died. He seemed like a broken man. When Zoey and Cole were heading to the hospital, the police were putting him into the back of the squad car after arresting him for kidnapping. Zoey didn't trust him. When she was alone with Nathan, he'd said his father should die and not quickly. She had no evidence he'd done anything wrong except not helping them more, and she worried he might not get in a lot of trouble.

Bryson promised to check-in, but Zoey had a feeling he planned to spend time with his child. Zoey couldn't wait to see the young girl again; she was the cutest thing. Cristin was quiet during the police questioning, only giving yes and no answers, but she never left Bryson's side. When the little girl looked at him, Zoey could see the love in her eyes.

The officers arrested the three men and Marcus for kidnapping.

For now, everything was excellent, and they didn't have to worry at night. Zoey couldn't wait until next month when she could talk with Kat about the shelter. Sitting with the bomb strapped to her, she'd realized how short life could be and wanted to do more and make an impact.

Cole had talked to Nathan earlier. He'd complained the doctors hadn't released him yet. She'd heard Cole trying to talk him into staying with them.

Zoey sat on the couch in the media room, her feet tucked under her as she leaned against Cole. The hospital had given her medication to help with the pain, but it always made her stomach hurt so badly, she refused to take it. The doctor had said the break was clean and didn't need any pins.

"How are you doing after having to shoot your mom?"

"Honestly?" Cole sighed. "She was a stranger to me. I hadn't seen her in years, and when I did live at home, she wasn't there or had someone else taking care of us."

"I know, but you can feel sad."

"I'm not." He ran his hand down the side of her arm.

"I'm glad we all made it out alive. So many things go through your mind when you have a bomb strapped to you."

"Like what?"

"I want to do the woman's shelter, but not only for women."

Cole wrapped his arm around her tighter. "You have the kindest heart. Most people would think about the trip they didn't get to go on or the place they didn't get to see. You worry about helping more people."

"I don't think I'm the first to have to go on the run," Zoey continued. "You mentioned Antonio runs a mercenary company. I wanted to know if he could help me find local men or women here who could help at the shelter. I don't want a place for them to hide, but a way out of their situation."

"I think that is a great idea." Cole gently swiped her hair behind her ear. "You know, next week, we are going to be extremely wealthy. I would like to use that money to help with your program."

Zoey stilled in his arms. She'd forgotten about the billion dollars. "That's your money."

"Wrong." He sighed. "That is my share of the Walker fortune. My family has done so much evil, I want to do good. One day, you will be my wife, so it is our money."

"I'm not even sure you heard your mother put a life insurance policy out on Nathan and planned to collect on top of trying to get your money. She was so greedy."

"Bryson cut off her lifeline. The banks would start coming after her if she couldn't pay the bills. Having houses like they did required staff and power and everything else. It's not cheap, and she wouldn't have the funds. That woman didn't have a motherly bone in her body. I'm surprised she had any kids at all."

"She was crazy. How did she hide it for so many years when you were younger?"

"No clue. But making Bryson's girlfriend and child go on the run…" Cole shook his head. "If I hadn't killed her, Bryson would've. Pretty sure he wished he could bring her back to life and kill her again. I was so fuckin' scared when I found out she took you and we couldn't find you right away. Damn. Don't ever disappear like that again."

Zoey tucked her hair behind her ear. "I will make sure to tell my kidnapper next time you don't approve." Zoey laughed. "I'm sure they will stop what they are doing and call you first."

Cole tickled Zoey's sides. "Don't be a smartass."

"On a serious note, thank you for coming for me."

"I know it will probably never happen again, but

would you be mad if I put a tracker on you," Cole asked.

"No." She didn't even need to think about the answer; it rolled off her tongue immediately. She had nothing to hide.

"Is it strange I think it's sexy as hell you will wear a tracker?"

"Yes." She giggled.

Cole slowly worked her shirt up her body, being careful not to move her arm too much. The cast still sent anger through him. He groaned when he noticed she didn't have on a bra. Leaning forward, he captured her nipple in his mouth. "God, you're perfect."

Lifting his head, he asked, "Did you change your lotion?"

She normally smelled like fresh flowers.

"Yes, it's pumpkin." She moaned as he took her nipple in his mouth.

"It smells good." Cole kissed between her breasts.

Cole slowly worked his way down her body, kissing her stomach and running his fingers across the top of her shorts. He slowly pulled them down her legs. He kissed the inside of her leg, and she ran her hand through his hair.

"Why are you torturing me?" she panted.

"I want to kiss every part of your body." He kissed above her hip bone and rolled her nipple between his fingers.

"The doctor said I was fine," Zoey whined. "I need you in me, or I might combust."

"Waiting makes the heart grow fonder," he whispered across her skin. Cole wanted to take his time and worship her body. The scare of almost losing her had him on edge, and he was trying to be slow, so he wouldn't hurt her.

Zoey shoved at his waistband. Cole jumped off the couch and quickly stripped. Cole climbed back on the sofa, positioning himself between her legs. He moved forward to slowly work himself into her. Zoey raised her hips and pressed forward, no longer waiting for Cole to slowly take her. She squeezed her inner muscles, almost sending him over the edge. He gritted his teeth, trying to keep control. She felt so good wrapped around him.

"Fuck." Cole breathed out.

"Faster, Cole." She urged him on.

Cole thrust forward. "You. Are. Mine."

Her eyes rolled back, and she called out his name. Cole reached between their bodies and pressed on her nub, extending Zoey's orgasm. He clenched his jaw, trying to stop himself from going over the edge.

Zoey reached up and squeezed her own nipple. Her touching herself was sexy as hell.

Cole pushed inside her a couple more times before feeling his balls tighten. “I love being inside you.” He rolled to the side and took her into his arms. “You make me the happiest man alive.”

“Thank you for coming for me.”

“I will always come for you.”

EPILOGUE – COLE

Cole looked across the pub at Zoey as she went to talk with Amanda and ask her to join them. Nathan sat next to Cole, watching everything around him. He'd been back for two months, and he hadn't talked about what happened while he was gone. When they asked, he said he didn't want to talk about it. Bryson was at the end of the table with his daughter on his lap and Cristin next to him.

Zoey was working with Kat to open an outreach center in San Antonio with the help of Tex and Antonio. She was interviewing retired vets to help protect women on the run. She was hoping to have the facility open in a couple months. Things were so much easier with money, and Cole had a lot of it. He didn't believe it until the lawyer called on his birthday and told him the steps he needed to take to access the funds.

It didn't matter he had the money—he still worked each day alongside his friend Ian. They had finally found an eight-unit apartment building. He enjoyed going to work each day and coming home to Zoey each night.

"I overheard you saying you're going to be in San Antonio for a while. How long are you going to stay?" Cole asked Nathan.

He didn't know how much his brother would say. Cole was fifty percent sure he was working another case. Nathan had thrown himself into CIA work since getting out of the hospital. Cole tried to talk him out of it, but nothing he said worked.

"I have a few things I need to take care of here this week, then I have an event in Paris next week," Nathan told Cole, but his eyes never left Amanda.

Amanda and Zoey were standing next to the bar, talking. Zoey had talked her into coming over to the house a few times for dinner, but she never stayed very long. There was more to her than she was letting on, and Cole worried she wouldn't ask for help when she really needed it.

"If you ever get sick of being an agent, I always have an opening working with Ian and me."

"I'll leave the manual labor to you," Nathan reassured him.

Cole watched as Zoey frowned at something Amanda said. He didn't like her unhappy.

Nathan must've noticed it also. "What do you know about the person Zoey is talking to?"

"She was medically discharged when her convoy went over an IUD. We've invited her over a few times, but she doesn't open up about much. I'm sure she is hiding something, but I don't know what it is. One day, I hope she will ask for help, because Zoey really likes her." Cole replied, looking down the table at his niece who'd fallen asleep on Bryson's lap.

Cole sat back and watched his friend and brother laugh. Bryson had taken to fatherhood quickly, and Cole loved seeing him happy. The door to the pub opened, and in walked a man he hadn't seen in years. The last time they were in the same room, Cole was in a hospital bed, recovering from his wounds. He blinked a few times as the man got closer.

"Tex?" Cole stood up and greeted the man. "Fuck, it's good to see you. I'm not even going to ask how you know where we were."

"Good to see you," Tex said.

Cole waved Zoey over.

"I'd like to introduce you to Zoey." Cole pulled her to his side. "Zoey, this is Tex."

"Thank you!" Zoey wrapped her arms around Tex. "I can never thank you for everything you did." She stepped back, and Tex waved off the thank you.

Ian walked over and hugged Tex, "Damn, it's been a long time. What brings you to Texas?"

"I was passing through on my way home and wanted to stop and see everyone."

Bryson walked over, carrying his sleeping daughter and holding Cristin's hand. He held out his hand and shook Tex's. "Nice to meet you, Tex. This is my daughter, Carly, and my girlfriend, Cristin."

Tex waved, and Nathan introduced himself.

Everyone sat around the table, and they pulled up another seat for Tex.

"Are Melody and the girls with you?" Ian asked.

"No, I had a quick trip out to see Wolf, and on my way back, I thought I would stop and see you guys."

"Make sure to tell Melody and the girls hi from us," Cole added.

"Maybe you guys can come out to Virginia when everything settles," Tex offered.

Zoey smiled. "I would love to come out there."

Tex and everyone sat around the table and chatted. Cole was enjoying being around friends. He planned to ask Zoey a question tonight, but he wanted to do it around the people who meant the most to him. He reached into his pocket and squeezed the black box he'd picked up from the jeweler a week ago. Zoey was his future, and he wanted her to be his wife. When he'd seen the bomb strapped to her body, he didn't know what he would do without her.

"Can I have everyone's attention for a moment?"

Everyone quieted down around them, and Cole stood, turning Zoey to the side. "Zoey, when we first met, you shot at me."

The people at the table laughed. Zoey rolled her eyes.

Cole continued, "I know you were scared and tired that day, but because of a chain of events, you ended up in my path. When you ran by me and out the door, I knew that second, I wanted to help you. When I saw how much you care for others, I wanted to know more about you. Over the past six months, I've watched you figure out how to help others. You turned the worst experience into something good." Cole got down on one knee. "There is no other person in the world I would want to spend my life with. Zoey Thomas, will you marry me?"

"Yes!" Zoey bent down, ignoring the ring, and wrapped her arms around Cole. She had tears running down her face.

Cole stood and captured her lips, wrapping his arms around her waist. When he pulled back, he put the emerald-cut diamond on her finger. "I love you, Zoey."

* * *

Nathan

"I'm so happy for them," Amanda said as she handed Nathan another beer. He'd gotten up and left the table to get a round of drinks and a few shots. He was happy for his brother, but he had so much anger inside, he was having a hard time showing it.

"He's lucky he found someone who won't stab him in the back." Nathan took a swig of his new beer. "How about a shot with me?"

Amanda eyed him for a second before she poured two shots of cinnamon whiskey. He clinked her glass. "Here's to being single."

"At least you have a choice in the matter," Amanda grumbled before downing the shot.

Cole watched the bartender for a moment. "You're hot as fuck."

"That's mean."

Nathan shrugged. "I don't know why you think that's mean. I think you're pretty."

"I thought you were making fun of me," Amanda answered.

"Nope." Nathan took another swig and watched her. "We all have scars... but you're hiding something."

"Why does everyone think I'm hiding something?"

"I don't think. I know."

Amanda narrowed her eyes. "I have nothing to hide."

Nathan leaned against the bar and whispered, "Then why are you looking at flights back to the Russia?"

"I don't know what you're talking about."

"Zoey seemed worried about you. So I've been watching you and I did some research. Last week, you booked a ticket back to Moscow."

Amanda shrugged. "Vacation."

"Bullshit. What if I said I could help you get your son back?"

"How?"

"You agree to be my wife, and I will get him back. You have three days to decide if you want to take my offer."

Click here to pre-order Unlocking Love. Find out if Amanda said yes.

ABOUT THE AUTHOR

Linzi Baxter lives in Orlando, Florida with her husband and lazy basset hound. She started writing when voices inside her head wouldn't stop talking until the story was told. When not at work as an IT Manager, Linzi enjoys writing action-packed romances that will take you to the edge of your seat.

She enjoys engaging her readers with strong, interesting characters that have complex and stimulating stories to tell. If you enjoy a little (or maybe a whole lot) of steam and spice, don't miss checking out White Hat Security series.

When not writing, Linzi enjoys reading, watching college sports (GO UCF Knights), and traveling to Europe. She loves hearing from her readers and can't wait to hear from you!

Sign up for Linzi Baxter's VIP Club for the latest news, giveaways, experts, and more.

It's completely free to sign up, and I will never spam you. It's easy to opt out at any time.

Click here to sign up!

facebook.com/authorlinzibaxter

twitter.com/authorbaxter

instagram.com/authorlinzibaxter

ALSO BY LINZI BAXTER

White Hat Security Series

Hacker Exposed

Royal Hacker

Misunderstood Hacker

Undercover Hacker

Hacker Revelation

Hacker Christmas

Hacker Salvation

Nova Satellite Security Series

(White Hat Security Spin Off)

Pursuing Phoenix

Pursuing Aries - March 31, 2020

Immortal Dragon

The Dragon's Psychic

The Dragon's Human

The Dragon's Mate - February 25, 2020

Montana Gold (Brotherhood Kindle World)

Grayson's Angel

Noah's Love

Bryson's Treasure - 2019

A Flipping Love Story (Badge of Honor World)

Unlocking Dreams

Unlocking Hope - 2019

Unlocking Love - May 2020

Siblings of the Underworld

Hell's Key

Hell's Future

Hell's Vacation 2020

Visit linzibaxter.com for more information and release dates.

Join Linzi Baxter Newsletter at Newsletter

There are many more books in this fan fiction world than listed here, for an up-to-date list go to www.AcesPress.com

You can also visit our Amazon page at:
http://www.amazon.com/author/operationalpha

Special Forces: Operation Alpha World

Christie Adams: Charity's Heart
Denise Agnew: Dangerous to Hold
Shauna Allen: Awakening Aubrey
Brynne Asher: Blackburn
Linzi Baxter: Unlocking Dreams
Jennifer Becker: Hiding Catherine
Alice Bello: Shadowing Milly
Heather Blair: Rescue Me
Anna Blakely: Rescuing Gracelynn
Amy Briggs: Saving Sarah
Julia Bright: Saving Lorelei
Victoria Bright: Surviving Savage
Cara Carnes: Protecting Mari
Kendra Mei Chailyn: Beast
Melissa Kay Clarke: Rescuing Annabeth
Samantha A. Cole: Handling Haven
Sue Coletta: Hacked
Melissa Combs: Gallant

Anne Conley: Redemption for Misty

KaLyn Cooper: Rescuing Melina

Liz Crowe: Marking Mariah

Sarah Curtis: Securing the Odds

Jordan Dane: Redemption for Avery

Tarina Deaton: Found in the Lost

KL Donn: Unraveling Love

Riley Edwards: Protecting Olivia

PJ Fiala: Defending Sophie

Nicole Flockton: Protecting Maria

Michele Gwynn: Rescuing Emma

Casey Hagen: Shielding Nebraska

EM Hayes: Gambling for Ashleigh

Desiree Holt: Protecting Maddie

Kathy Ivan: Saving Sarah

Jesse Jacobson: Protecting Honor

Silver James: Rescue Moon

Becca Jameson: Saving Sofia

Kate Kinsley: Protecting Ava

Heather Long: Securing Arizona

Gennita Low: No Protection

Kirsten Lynn: Joining Forces for Jesse

Margaret Madigan: Bang for the Buck

Kimberly McGath: The Predecessor

Rachel McNeely: The SEAL's Surprise Baby

KD Michaels: Saving Laura

Wren Michaels: The Fox & The Hound
Kat Mizera: Protecting Bobbi
Mary B Moore: Force Protection
LeTeisha Newton: Protecting Butterfly
Angela Nicole: Protecting the Donna
MJ Nightingale: Protecting Beauty
Sarah O'Rourke: Saving Liberty
Victoria Paige: Reclaiming Izabel
Anne L. Parks: Mason
Debra Parmley: Protecting Pippa
Lainey Reese: Protecting New York
TL Reeve and Michele Ryan: Extracting Mateo
Elena M. Reyes: Keeping Ava
Angela Rush: Charlotte
Rose Smith: Saving Satin
Jenika Snow: Protecting Lily
Lynn St. James: SEAL's Spitfire
Dee Stewart: Conner
Harley Stone: Rescuing Mercy
Jen Talty: Burning Desire
Megan Vernon: Protecting Us

Police and Fire: Operation Alpha World

Freya Barker: Burning for Autumn
KaLyn Cooper: Justice for Gwen
Aspen Drake: Sheltering Emma

Deanndra Hall: Shelter for Sharla

Barb Han: Kace

CM Steele: Guarding Hope

Reina Torres: Justice for Sloane

Stacey Wilk: Stage Fright

As you know, this book included at least one character from Susan Stoker's books. To check out more, see below.

SEAL of Protection: Legacy Series

Securing Caite

Securing Brenae (novella)

Securing Sidney

Securing Piper

Securing Zoey (Jan 2020)

Securing Avery (May 2020)

Securing Kalee (Sept 2020)

Delta Team Two Series

Shielding Gillian (Apr 2020)

Shielding Kinley (Aug 2020)

Shielding Aspen (Oct 2020)

Shielding Riley (TBA)

Shielding Devyn (TBA)

Shielding Ember (TBA)

Shielding Sierra (TBA)

Delta Force Heroes Series

Rescuing Rayne (FREE!)

Rescuing Aimee (novella)
Rescuing Emily
Rescuing Harley
Marrying Emily (novella)
Rescuing Kassie
Rescuing Bryn
Rescuing Casey
Rescuing Sadie (novella)
Rescuing Wendy
Rescuing Mary
Rescuing Macie (Novella)

Badge of Honor: Texas Heroes Series

Justice for Mackenzie (FREE!)
Justice for Mickie
Justice for Corrie
Justice for Laine (novella)
Shelter for Elizabeth
Justice for Boone
Shelter for Adeline
Shelter for Sophie
Justice for Erin
Justice for Milena
Shelter for Blythe
Justice for Hope
Shelter for Quinn

Shelter for Koren
Shelter for Penelope

SEAL of Protection Series

Protecting Caroline (FREE!)
Protecting Alabama
Protecting Fiona
Marrying Caroline (novella)
Protecting Summer
Protecting Cheyenne
Protecting Jessyka
Protecting Julie (novella)
Protecting Melody
Protecting the Future
Protecting Kiera (novella)
Protecting Alabama's Kids (novella)
Protecting Dakota

New York Times, USA Today and *Wall Street Journal* Bestselling Author Susan Stoker has a heart as big as the state of Tennessee where she lives, but this all American girl has also spent the last fourteen years living in Missouri, California, Colorado, Indiana, and Texas. She's married to a retired Army man who now gets to follow *her* around the country.

www.stokeraces.com
www.AcesPress.com
susan@stokeraces.com

Made in the USA
Monee, IL
21 December 2019

19322477R00128